Advance Reader Copy

You are viewing an Advance Reader Copy of this title. As there may be corrections, deletions, or other changes before publication, please check with the publisher or refer to the finished book before quoting in a review. Price and publication date are subject to change

Not for Resale

High

Mary Sullivan

Fitzroy Books

Published by Fitzroy Books
An imprint of
Regal House Publishing, LLC
Raleigh, NC 27612

https://fitzroybooks.com

Printed in the United States of America

ISBN -13 (paperback): 9781646031702
ISBN -13 (epub): 9781646031719
Library of Congress Control Number:

Interior and cover design by Lafayette & Greene
Cover images © by C.B. Royal

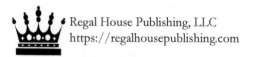

Regal House Publishing, LLC
https://regalhousepublishing.com

Printed in the United States of America

For all those who choose to hold fast to dreams.

And for my mother, who has always been my light.

Author's Note

Ceti
is a single star
in the constellation
Cetus
that is spectrally similar
to the Sun.

Happy

Sometimes I'm so high
it's like I live in the clouds,
like I own the world.

Today from our nineteenth floor
I can hardly see my old school field
where the boys are playing soccer
                                        in all the fog,
but I bet Will's there.
I got my Messi ball and my cleats,
and I'm floating out the door
before Foxface gets here.

Take the stairs, all nineteen flights,
smelling laundry detergent and piss,
thinking someone should fix the lights.
Then run past the front desk, along the river
till I get to the game.
Dribble down the sideline,
trying not to stare.
Trying not to breathe
too hard.
Already had my practice,
now I roll my ball into the air
like I got all day.

Finally, Will goes,
"Hey, Ceti, wanna play?"

"Wassup with that?" Tyler whines.

"Shut up.
Just cuz she's better than you."

"You can have her."
Tyler comes after me hard,
like he's gonna slide tackle me.
I jump over him, pass the ball outside to Will.
He sends it back, one touch. I'm about to cross it
when Tyler cuts
me
down
and steals the ball.
I catch up to him
and flick the ball back to our goalie,
who punts it halfway down the field.

I'm happy when I'm playing.
Mom didn't name me after a star
for nothing. But I don't wanna think
about her or Foxface right now,
only about the next goal.
I wanna score.

Light rain is coming down,
and the ground is soft.
I'm running through the clouds,
cutting down the side,
dribbling around them, rolling it back.
Next goal wins, and I want this one.
I need it more than they do.
Mom hasn't been able to make it
to any of my games yet—
maybe the quarter finals
on Saturday.

Will says, "You get this
and I owe you Tasty Burger."

"Yeah?"

"Yeah."

Only thing that matters is me
and the ball
and the next goal.
I send one into space
between Will and the goalie.
He sprints and tips it in so sweetly.
Then throws his head back,
shaking his ridiculous, floppy hair.
Grabs me close enough
to smell his sweat and heat.
Something inside me melts—
I catch it in his dark eyes too,
like in that second
we could go from friends
to something else.
It feels so good
I think I'm gonna
die.

After he lets go
I still feel the warmth
where his fingers were.
Makes me want it
all over again.

Plays Khalid on his phone.
Nothing feels better than—

Says, "See you later, okay?"

"Yeah." Wanna say, *when*?
I've only been waiting forever.
He has no idea how happy I am
right now.
And someone left an Orange Crush on the sidelines.
I grab it. Drink down the sweet sparkle
in one long gulp.

Tyler goes, "Who's your daddy?"

Don't know if he's talking to me.
It's after-school pick-up time,
and no one's collecting me,
especially Foxface.
He'll never be my daddy.

A man in a suit stops, says,
"You're good."

"Thanks."

"I used to play—" He laughs.
"About a million years ago.
Heard the girls team made the finals—"

"Yeah, we're gonna win, too,"
I tell him.

A kid yells from the playground, "Daddy!"
Arms out, running like mad.

A flash of light crosses the sky,
bright in the dark November—

got to check Mom *now.*
I snag my ball, sky blue with darker jags
like bird wings,
and take off
toward home.

Fool to Cry

I fly past Will. Can't wait today,
even though he lives on the seventh floor
                    of our building.
He's with his sophomore friends
and I'm only in ninth.
Anyway, I love shooting up in the elevator.
Mom used to say, "Ceti, you're not a falling star,
you're a shooting star. Remember that."
No one's in the hallway
so I boot my ball down the old brown carpet,
do a fake around the defender,
roll back,
and *score*!

Score again—Mom's home and Foxface isn't.
But she's not moving.
I run to her,
put my head on her chest
to hear her heart
beating.
A half-eaten Dunkin' Donut with sprinkles
rises slowly up
and down
on her gray T-shirt.
                "Mom, are you good?"

She looks up with glazed eyes
and smiles.
"Sorry, Ceti babe, I forgot
to go to the store today."

Her eyes are like the rain
streaming down our windows,
and she's the glass.
I don't want her to break.

"It's okay, I can get something to eat."

In the kitchen,
I'll find a spoon in the sink,
a ball of tin foil and a needle in the trash.

She's crying and crying now.

I want to say,
Why don't you do something instead,
but at least
she's still
here.

Paint It Black

When Mom starts shivering
I go to her closet for a sweater.
I don't know why the inside of her door
                is painted red,
but it's been like that since we moved in.
She has a poster tacked up of "Paint It Black"
when Brian Jones, her favorite Rolling Stone,
was in the band.

We started listening
after Mom bought the red pick-up truck,
with Stones CDs in the glove compartment.
We played them over and over,
the music filling up the space between us—
her in the driver's seat
and me next to her, reclined all the way.
If her back didn't hurt.
she'd hold my hand
                until I fell asleep.

I pick up Mom's black sweater
from the dirty clothes scattered across her floor,
make-up, bottles stuffed with cigarettes,
tinfoil, a lighter, a tub of Vaseline.
When I used to sleep in here
the sheets were clean and white,
not gray and matted with her long honey hair
and his short dark ones.
And it didn't smell gross
like throw-up and smoke.

A silver frame peeks out
from a pile of junk in the closet.
The Disney castle looms
behind us like a fake background.
It doesn't even look like us—
Mom in her bikini top and jean shorts
and me with two braids,
just like any other six-year-old kid
in Florida.
I slide the picture
in my hoodie
and shut the closet door.
The wooden edges
are coated with black splotches—
dark heart shapes in the corners,
creeping over the red,
like she's painting her door black.

Get Off of My Cloud

I come out with Mom's sweater
right as Foxface comes in.
I'm not supposed to be in their room.
I look down so he can't see my eyes.
But he's in a good mood, singing along,
Hey, hey you, you
get off of my —

He tosses his MAGA cap onto the couch
next to Mom, slouches beside her,
his head ted so I can see the whole
tattoo on his neck—
an orange fox with its mouth open,
glistening sharp teeth,
yellow eyes snarling.
A black and white skull
on top of this. Other skulls
are tattooed on his fingers,
one like the ring
Keith Richards wears.
The gold cross in his left ear
is the only religious thing about Foxface.
Protection from evil, he says.
Right?

I think the song is stuck
cuz it's playing over and over.
And now she's singing and sort of dancing
but not really. More like falling—
but at least she's not crying anymore.

Don't know if I can call what Foxface is doing *dancing.*
His arms are swinging like some crazy puppet
and his body's like a beater going around
        and around.
Hey, hey
        you, you—
The words are puffs of smoke
that swirl up to the ceiling and disappear.

        Her hair's a greasy tangle
and she smells so bad.
Maybe that's why she pulls off her pants
so all she has on is her gray T-shirt
and sweater barely covering her.
Foxface grabs her, laughing.

Before they bring me down
I got to go
        jump on my own cloud.
I grab my Messi ball
and run out the door
down the stairs again.

Back to school to practice

cuz I'm gonna be so good

she'll stay

    clean.

Indian Girl

When I was five Mom got me a pair of moccasins
with two layers of fringe,
and a thunderbird in red, white, and black beads.
She said they'd give me supernatural power.
And I believed her.

At night she'd sing me to sleep,
little Indian girl, little Indian girl
little Indian girl—

I wore my hair in a long braid
down my back and told everyone
I could turn into a thunderbird.
I raced them through the playground
and flew past them every time.

"Why don't you have sneakers?"
they asked.

"Because I'm an Indian,"
I said.

"Is that why you smell?"
They laughed and laughed.
"Because you live in a teepee?
A peepee!"

"No, I don't. I live in my truck."

They frowned. "What do you mean,

you live in your truck?"

"It's red," I said.
"It's our space capsule."

When I told Mom, she said,
"Hey, little Indian girl, don't tell anyone
else that. Don't tell them
anything."

"Am I really an Indian girl?"

"Yeah, and this is Fiery Red Cloud."
She patted the dashboard.

"Where's my dad?" I asked.
"Is he an Indian?"

"I don't know where the hell he is."
She poured a glass of wine,
her sleeping medicine,
and wrapped another blanket
around me.

"What about Gramps?
Is he an Indian?"

She laughed so hard she spit her wine out.
"Yup, that's him—soccer-playing Indian Gramps!"

Rain fell on the roof
like the steady thrumming
of a drum.
Outside, two men with blankets
scrambled through the parking lot

for a doorway.

“We’re lucky
we’re not out there.
Right, Mom?”

“That’s right, babe.
We’re lucky.”
She turned the heat on full blast
until I fell asleep, listening to her singing
in a whisper,
“*Lesson number one*
you learn when you’re young—”
Rain streamed down our windows.
“*Life just goes on and on—*”

Indian Girl #2

One night our truck was towed,
so Mom got us a blanket and we rolled up
on the wet grass in the school park.
She rolled a smoke and stared at the sky,
puffing away, not saying anything,
filling the night with a skunky smell.

"Mom?"

"Not now, Ceti.
I'm thinking."
Embers sparkled between her fingers like fireflies.
"Thinking how to get us some cash.
Go to sleep, babe."

In the middle of the night, I woke
and she wasn't there. I was so cold
and hungry my insides hurt.
I rolled
into a ball
and waited
for the light.
I thought,
What if she doesn't come back?
Could I even find Gramps
in Roosevelt Towers?

After the *looooooooooooooooonnnnnnnggggggggggest* time,
pink strips
spread through

my blanket,
and she was there again.
I held on to her so tight,
she said, “Don’t strangle me, Ceti.
Not when I got a pocket of Freedom right here.”
She smiled, patting her jeans pocket.
“Let’s get something to eat.”

Indian Girl #3

We lived in Mom's truck till it was too cold.
Then we moved back to the shelter by Gramps.

He cried
when I walked into his room
at Roosevelt Towers,
His face crumpled
and his shoulders were shaking
so much he couldn't talk.
Then he wiped his face
and pointed at the TV.
"Stay, Ceti,
and watch with me.
Messi's like playing with fire.
You never know which way he's going.
Sees at least four plays ahead."
His words shook out of his mouth
and he cried again,
so I held his face
between my hands
and looked into his cloudy eyes.

"Here I am, Gramps.
I'm here now."

It was like a storm was moving through him.
"Don't leave like that again, okay?
You're everything—"

I said, "I won't, Gramps. I'll stay.
Promise."

Play with Fire

Thanks to Gramps,
I got Messi's first-touch down.
If I had a phone, I'd text Will right now
to see if he could kick the ball around with me.
He'd be Ronaldo and I'd be Messi,
the best soccer player in the world.
Will would say, "Hate to tell you,
but Ronaldo gets more goals,"
and he'd try to steal the ball—
but I'd trick him out.
Sometimes I don't even touch
the ball, just dodge right, left,
and fly by.

I'd tell Will, "Your boy's a machine—
doesn't have Messi's vision."

"He's way taller. Like me."
Will would push me from the side.

"He's too flashy—
GOOOAAALLL!"

"Better at heading too," Will'd say.

"Better at having a big head, yeah."
I'd dribble by him
again.

Gramps was my best coach.

Every weekend after we got back
I'd watch games with him at Roosevelt.
He said, "I'm going to teach you to read soccer
by watching every play."
He'd pick me up at the shelter
and take me to the town league practice.
When Mom came to my games, she'd tell me,
"Ceti, you're the best soccer player in the world!"

Even if she's not saying it anymore,
she can't take back what she's already given me.
And now *I'm* playing with fire.

Night's cool
and the stars are barely visible,
but I'm dreaming anyway—
of scoring, winning—

and Will.

Did he mean it today?
Does he like

me?

I got him,
the finals,
the whole sky—
no one's gonna shoot me down tonight—
ball goes *smack, smack, smack*—
that one's for Foxface.

Under My Thumb

Foxface is her zookeeper, the man
with the white powder
who says he'll stop the mad
itching, the stomach pains,
the diarrhea and vomiting,
the crying, the scabbing
up and down her arms,
teeth turning dark yellow,
the rotten smell.
Foxface will fix her,
make her beautiful again.
After the doctor stopped Mom's prescription,
and she lost her waitressing job,
Foxface became her new doctor.
Instead of little happy pills she got

Smack	Smack	Smack	Smack
Snow	Horse	Dope	Junk
White Lady	Brown Sugar	Junk	Snow
Smack	Snow	White Stuff	Skag
Skag	White Girl	Dragon	Smack
Brown Sugar	Snow	White Nurse	Horse
Dragon	White Girl	White Horse	Big H

The stuff that keeps her trapped.

I kick my ball
against the wall
smack.

Messi says,
You have to fight
for your dream.
You have to sacrifice
and work hard for it.
I wrote that on my ball
in Sharpie so I wouldn't forget it.
Most of the letters
have been kicked off.
They're only ghost words,
but I know they're there.

I pick up my ball and hold it close.
Tell myself
we're going to win
the States—we have to
cuz I don't know
what else to do.

There's gotta be something bigger
than this.

She's a Rainbow

I remember when
she used to pick me
up from school.
All tall and willowy
like she was hanging
from the sky, she was
like a rainbow spreading
her color everywhere:

Her blue coat flapping
open in the breeze,
her honey hair swinging
across her back, her green eyes
shadowed with turquoise
and her lips bright pink.
In the spring she'd wear
a yellow flower tucked behind her ear,
and in the winter red jeans
and silver snakeskin boots.
Heads turned as she walked
down the street
toward me.

And I'd run
into her arms
like I could hold on
to all the colors
of her rainbow.

Faraway Eyes

I've been getting
everywhere by myself
for years.
And now
her rainbow
is more like the grayish-brown
of all the colors
puddled together.
Even her green eyes
are cloudy
and faraway,
especially when Foxface
is there.
It's like
he took
her color
away.

I make a target
on the brick wall and kick
that ball as hard as I can
smack into his pointy nose
and chin, eyes like slits.
Even his beard is pointy.
But his body
is soft and spongy.
I kick harder
with my right foot
then left, smashing
his stupid face
over and over.

Heaven

If I had a phone, I could call Ruby.
Her mom would make me
hot chocolate with whipped cream,
and we could play Heaven on her trampoline.
Take turns bouncing each other,
whoever goes the highest wins.
When I jump it's like flying
so high into the sky
into nothingness
that nothing can hold
me down. At Ruby's
it's like nothing's
ever going to hurt me.

Haven't been over since school started.
Soccer's every day,
and Ruby's taking dance now.
And she's got all these new friends
I don't know.
She's still my best friend,
but going over there
makes going home
like hell.

Sister Morphine

On the way back
the fog has cleared
enough so I can see
a shape on our porch
on the nineteenth floor,
leaning over the railing.
She can't

jump—

I stop breathing—
I clutch my ball,
sprint to the lobby,
shoot up to number nineteen,
run down the hallway.

Mom.

I breathe. In.
And.
Out.

She's the color of a bruise—
her eyes, skin, arms, legs—
skinny like the stick figures
I used to draw.

"Mom, are you okay?"

"Yeah, Ceti.

Things aren't what they seem."
Her smile is gray and skinny too.

"Do you want me to wash your hair?
I can start a bath?"

She leans toward me and says,
"If you get me some money
from one of those rich kids
at school who have everything, or—"
She snatches my arm too tight.
"Take their phone so we can sell it.
They won't even miss it.
They'll just get a new one."
She's talking too fast,
her eyes blazed.

"Okay," I say carefully.
"Will you take a bath?"

She takes my face in her hands.
"Ceti, you could be happy with me."
She puts her tiny bag of gray powder
on the table in front of me.

No. No. No. No.

Can't find my breath.
I turn away. Whisper,
"I have school tomorrow.
And soccer."

Her eyes narrow. "You think
you're better than me, Ceti?"
Soft and hard, hard and soft.

"Why don't you have a face, Ceti?"

My face is gray and hollow,
my teeth are brownish yellow,
I'm scabbed, greasy, filthy—
I have to check the mirror
fast.

I move past that—
and see myself—my skin is smooth,
and I have hazel eyes, same nose and ears,
Mom's honey hair
with long choppy bangs—
I *do* have a face.

"I'm good," I say slowly.

She says, "Leave me alone, Ceti.
Get away from me."

I can blame Foxface
for the rest of my life,

but she chose this.

I tell myself, *Never never, never—*

"You'll cave one day," she calls back.
"When the world starts falling around you,
you'll cave."
Her laughter circles the apartment,

circles my face.

You Got the Silver

I leave her alone.
What else am I gonna do—
pick her up and carry her into the tub?
I probably could—she's so skinny.
But I never saw that—something like hate—
in her eyes before. Makes me hate her
and everything else. Makes my stomach hurt
even more.
                    I wish it were breakfast time
and I could go to school and eat.
I take my books out of my bag
and spread them across my bed.
A Hershey Bar spills out.
                                        No note
but I know it's from Ruby.
I open it and put a square on my tongue.
I want to let it melt slowly
so it'll last. Instead,
I eat the whole bar in seconds.
Nothing ever tasted so good.
Sometimes I think I could
tell Ruby stuff, but what if she told
someone else?

                    If anyone found out,
they'd take Mom away for good.
That's what Mom said.

I fall asleep, but in the middle of the night
I hear someone crying softly.

I can't see anything, but I know
someone's here.
Cold sucks under my skin.
Don't hurt me, don't make me get high,
please. Please.

I pretend I'm asleep,
sprawled out over
my Spanish homework.

When my eyes get used to the light
I see Mom on the floor, her back against
the wall. She cries in a whisper, "Sorry, Ceti.
I'm going to be better, babe.
You're my gold, babe.
We have a pact."

I make a fist over the scars on my palm.
Don't move.
                                        Don't move.
The conjugations of *ser* and *estar*
are running under my wet cheek.
Both mean "to be," but *ser* is permanent
                                        and *estar* is temporary.
                                        What is she?
I should have said I'd get her some money.
I shouldn't have hated her—*I hate that*
                                        in me.

Loving Cup

Practice ends early
since tomorrow
is game day.
No suicides today.
We make a chain,
holding hands
and yell, "Go Falcons!"
I hold on tighter,
          their hands warm in mine.
We huddle in.
Coach asks us,
Who's going to win?
Who we going to beat?
When're we gonna do it?

Winning seems so easy
when you're on a team.
The Varsity girls are nice,
but they're mostly juniors and seniors,
one sophomore, and me.
They're making plans
for Friday night.
          I'm about to take off
when Coach calls me back.
She pushes her Red Sox cap down,
swings her ponytail around
to face me.

"Too healthy," Mom said about Coach
the one time she picked me up.

She wasn't happy when Coach gave me
her daughter's old cleats
and shin guards either.

Coach says, "Ceti, I got some news for you."
All sweaty and raggedy,
I wipe my face with the end
of my ripped T-shirt and wait.

"You know that U.S. scout I mentioned?"
Coach is always tough
and all about soccer,
but right now her eyes are glassy
and she can't hold in
her smile.

up.
The sky is swirling, the ground is tilting
I pull my gray socks up
and say, "Yeah, the scout you told me about."

"Well, she's coming to watch
you play."

My head starts buzzing.
"What's that mean?"

"It means we'll have to get you some new cleats."
She laughs a little.

"I'm going to get some tomorrow."
I've been saving up, and the pair of Messis I need
just went on sale.

"Good. Now think Nationals," she says.
"You have to be fifteen."

I nod and hold my lucky ball.
"I'm almost fifteen."

"I know." Her smile's so big,
it's like a cup and she's offering me a drink.
She's not an idiot—she says,
"Everything's paid for. It's only the beginning.
Do you know how many girls are offered this?"

I shake my head.

"About a hundred in the whole country,
and you're one of the youngest."
She's smiling, and I'm so thirsty.
"You've worked hard, Ceti.
I see you running and playing after practice.
You deserve this."

"I do?"

Lines fold around her eyes
and mouth. Does she mean it?
She says, "Yes, you do."

This beautiful buzz lifts me,
humming and singing,
and it's like I'm drinking
the sky I'm so high.
I say it to myself, *Nationals*
Nationals
Nationals—
Not sure exactly what it means
yet, but there's power in there
somewhere.

I can do this for real.
I hold up my ball—

just one little drink.

Shine a Light

I'm kicking my ball
against the brick wall
behind school when
Ruby swings over,
her hair a curly halo
around her face.
She's with Natasha and Grace.
"Wanna sleep over tonight?
I got Cheetos."

"Can't. Tomorrow's
game day."

"Right," she says.

Did she actually forget—
or did she really *want* me to sleep over
with her new friends?

"I'll be there. Good luck,"
she says with a quick hug.

"Thanks."
I want to tell her about the scout—
I mean, Ruby's been my best friend since fourth grade
when she chose me to be on her soccer team.
"You're intrepid," she said then.

"What's *that*?" I said.

"It means you're not afraid of things."

But I am afraid—that's what she didn't see.

They're already heading down the sidewalk,
hips swaying, hair swishing,
fearless.

Ruby's mom was in some fancy rehab
for drinking, but I can't tell Ruby how bad
it is for me. Everything looks different
when you're rich.
You go somewhere expensive
and come back better.
I bet Ruby's mom never
tried to get Ruby to drink.
And our place could fit inside
hers at least five times.

If I was invited to Nationals,
how could I just go?
Last night I thought Mom
was going to   jump.

I try not to think
about anything
besides kicking
the ball
against the wall
and soaking in the sun,
waiting
for everyone
to go somewhere
else.

"Hey." Will traps my ball.
"Busy?"

Don't say, don't say, don't say.
"Just daydreaming about that shot
Messi took from the fifty."

"Yeah, I been there." He nods.
"Wanna go to Tasty?"

I go, "Right, you owe me, don't you?"

"Yeah," he says.

He smells so good, all salty and sweet, I laugh.

"What's so funny?"

"Nothing."

He waits.

I don't move.

"Well?"

I *can't* move.

There's a line of sweat on his forehead
when he grabs my hand and pulls me forward.
But I'm the one who's shaking.
I can't get that close—
it's easier to be alone—
cuz I might lose
him
too.

We start walking and even though
he lets my hand go,
it's still burning.

He says, "You have no idea how good it was
to beat those guys the other day."
When he smiles
it's like a light shining
down on me,
warm as the late afternoon sun,
and his teeth are so white
against his perfect brown skin
I almost cry.
He puts his arm across my shoulder.
"Hey, don't worry,"
he says and pulls me in so I can hear
Post Malone singing, *I'm falling*
but everyone falls—
through his AirPods.

Dance Little Sister Dance

The jukebox at Tasty Burger is playing—
Will twists his body, knee out, hips loose.
Just for a second
but sometimes that's all it takes.
I smile so big I think my face is gonna break
off.

I say, "My mom and I used to dance to this.
People used to think I was her little sister."
They never ask that anymore—

"How's she doing? Haven't seen her in a while."
He orders two cheeseburgers and fries.

I shrug. "She has a really lame boyfriend."

"The guy with the tattoo and beard?"

"Yup. Foxface."

"What's he do that's so bad?"

"Um—
it's like he's holding her
down, you know."

"Yeah."

Feels good to hear someone say that.
Just *yeah.*

Don't wanna think about anything
except hot salty fries covered in ketchup
and the music on the jukebox,
but I'm drifting back
to a bunch of summers ago
when the AC wasn't working
and Mom and I went to the pool.
After, we kept our wet bikinis on
and danced around the apartment, screaming,
"Dance little sister, dance!"
She was shaking all over the living room,
even on the couch and the coffee table.
It was just me and her
in our citadel,
as we used to call it.

"Ready for your game?" Will asks.
His hair is a crazy tangle going in every direction
and his eyes are so dark I can see myself in there.

Got to look away.
"Yup."

"I'll be there."

I swallow.
"Cool."

We eat without talking.
When I pop the last fry in,
Will says, "Better go."

"That was so good.
Must be my lucky day."
After I say it,

I want to take it
back.

But he doesn't laugh,
just looks a little longer
at me,

and then we start back home
along the river.
Sun's already gone down
when we get to the circle of trees
in the courtyard.
In the elevator before he gets off
on the seventh floor, he leans toward me.
"Hey, I'll see you soon."
His chin brushes my cheek,
his arms circle me, holding me close,
and I swear I'm gonna explode,
like shatter into pieces—
I want more.
He sticks his foot out to hold the elevator door,
sways me side to side.
It's all way too
weird.

I don't want him to let go.
No one's touched
me
for so long.

"You good?" He steps into the hallway,
his hand stopping the elevator.

"Yeah, I'm good,"
I say, not pressing the button going up.

"Your birthday's coming up."

"Yeah. The big one five."
I know he just turned sixteen,
but how does he know about me?

.
"Whattya want?"

"To stop time." Thinking, *like right now.*

He laughs. "Good luck with that one."

I float up
the next twelve floors
like I'm made of feathers.

Mother's Little Helper

All these good supper smells are seeping out
of the doors I pass. I stop in front of one
that's like the Hawaiian chicken
at Gramp's assisted living.
Take a deep breath
of sweet and sour.
Last time I saw him, he said,
"Pretty soon I'll have more hair on my face
than on my head."

I laughed.

"Ceti—" he said.

"I know," I said.

His gray-blue eyes were watery.

"You love me more
than all the stars in the sky."

"That's right. Don't you forget it either, Ceti girl."

I saw myself in those watery eyes then,
and again the night we left New York
on a Peter Pan bus.
When I asked Mom where
we were going,
she pointed.
"That way."

Every time I asked her
when
we'd see
Gramps
again,
she'd say,
"Someday,
little Indian girl."
Until I stopped asking.

At night she sang
Life just goes on and on
getting harder—

Brown sugar pineapple and chicken on rice
smells so good.
I miss
him
so
much.

When I get to our door
I remember one more thing
I don't wanna—

turn my hand over
            to see
white lines
            crisscrossing
the center of my palm.

Happened after that time
we were dancing
like crazy on the furniture,

her bikini top half off,
dancing till she crashed
and started crying,
saying it was all
too much.
"It hurts, Ceti! Did you hear me?
I need my meds! I need more—"
She rolled off the couch,
banging her head on the floor.
"Well, help me, Ceti.
Are you just gonna stand there?"

"What should I do?"

"I need a drink.
Get me a beer, babe.
I hit my freakin' head."

She drank it down in seconds.
"Another."

"They're gone."

She slammed the empty bottle beside her,
shattering glass across the floor,
the broken neck of the bottle
still in her fist,
dripping red.

"It hurts, Ceti. Do you even care?"

"Yes, Mom."

"Do you want to know what it feels like?"
She came toward me.

I backed away,
but she grabbed my hand.
"We have to make a pact.
Just you and me."
Then she sliced into the meaty
center of my palm
with the edge of glass—
slice, slice, slice—
quick mad strokes
like clean heat
searing through me.
I screamed
when blood
streamed out
like a river.

"You and me, Ceti,
for*ever*."
And she pressed
her palm to mine,
blood to blood.

I'd never been scared of her before,
but I ran and slid under my bed.
She couldn't fit under there,
so she rolled on the floor next to me,
crying.
"I'm sorry, Ceti. You're all I have.
I'm doing this for you."

I squeezed my hand into a ball
and watched her turn away,
screeching,
"I need some goddamn more of these!"
She threw her empty prescription bottle

across the room.
“It’s her fault! She started me
on freakin’ pills when I was eight!”

Now, in the hallway
outside our apartment,
I need to get back
to a good place fast:
rewind that last hour and a half
with Will—
stop, and rewind
again.

Wild Horses

I push open the door and step inside.
Supper's not exactly cooking on the stove,
but at least they're not scratching or twitching
or too whacked-out happy,
or in the bathroom getting sick—
they're watching *The Walking Dead*.
Mom and Foxface are curled up together
on the couch, watching zombies
rip chunks of flesh out of a horse.
Mom says, "Hey, babe, how's things?"

"Good," I say.
"How can you watch this?"

They barely lift their eyes from the screen
like their normal is zombie-normal.

Not me.
I'm a survivor.

In my room, I pick up my horse statue.
When I turned five, she said,
"Someday I'll get you a real horse,
little Indian girl."

I kept that horse next to me
every night since.
I used to dream
I was galloping so fast
I had to hold

onto its mane.
          Now I dream
          about galloping
          down the soccer field
          toward the goal.
          Time is running out,
          game's almost over,
          and I gotta score.
          Before I shoot,
          I look around
          to see if she's there,
          watching me.

Someday, right?
The first time I saw her strung out
I knew my someday was a long way
away.

In the middle of the night I wake.
She's not in the room, but I hear her
somewhere calling me in a whisper,
"Hey, Ceti, let's do some living
after we die."

As Tears Go By

The first time
I knew about Mom
we were at the school park.

Ruby and I were playing,
and I didn't realize it was raining
till I saw Mom's face.
She waved to us
and ducked under
the doorway of a classroom.

We jumped off the swings,
and ran over to Mom,
who stepped into a stream
of rain dripping from the roof.
Water splashed all over her face
and the front of her T-shirt.
She laughed, calling,
"I love you, Ceti,
I love you!"
The hollow sounds hung
in the air, then disappeared
in the sound of rain
hitting the ground.

Mom dried off enough
to light a rolled-up cigarette.
It sizzled when she drew in smoke.
"Tell me you love me, Ceti.
Say you love me. Say it, Ceti."

Ruby looked from me
to Mom. I didn't say anything.
I was nine and I knew something
was wrong.
                    We watched
the cigarette burn down to her fingers.
The hairs on her skin shriveled into nothing.
It smelled like hamburger frying.

Ruby screamed, then slapped the cigarette
out of Mom's hand, into a puddle.
Mom laughed.
"Don't worry, it didn't hurt.
I didn't even feel it."
Rain was pouring
out of her eyes.

                    I said, "Mom, where are you?"

"Here I am," she sang. "I'm so happy,
Ceti."

Ruby was staring at Mom's arm.
Gray blue bruises blossomed
on her veins like black flowers
on a dark path.

Heartbreaker

Today is quarter finals at home.
Last day in the cleats Coach gave me.
Right after the game I'm heading to Olympia Sports
for the best soccer cleats in the world—
Adidas Messis in shock blue
and silver metallic,
on sale for forty-eight ninety-five
or ten times feeding Mrs. Johnson's cat.
Just imagining those cleats on my feet
makes me bullet one in from the eighteen.
I tap another one coming
across the center into the net.
Then dodge past the defender
and shoot it into the corner.
My team huddles around me.
Will is on the sidelines,
and Ruby too.

I wish I wish I wish
Gramps could see me now.

At half-time Coach says,
"Hey, girl-on-fire, nice job out there.
I'm proud of you."

I can't help it. A WALL
goes up around me
She doesn't know anything about me.
I move to the outside of our circle.
Coach pushes her baseball cap down,

squats in front of us, and gets all serious
about our defense holding them off.
Even though this team's a piece of cake.
—fluffy vanilla.
I'm taking this cake
and eating it in one bite.

Orange slices finally make their way to me.
I stuff in as many as I can.
Sometimes I wonder what it'd be like
to have a mom who cuts oranges
into neat wedges
for the whole team.

We win, and they crowd around me.
Then Ruby spins me around
and says, "Let anyone else score much?"
And Will goes, "Sweet game, Ceti.
See you later?"

I'm on top of the world,
number one on someone's list.
Coach is happy.
Semifinals is in four days,
finals in seven,
when the scout will be there.
"Where's your mom?" Coach says.
Meaning *she should be here*—

I am holding on to this high—
time to fly—
like I can't hear them
calling my name.
Gotta get my Messis.
Sale is today only.

Sail down the sidewalk,
seeing myself in those blue and silver cleats—
no more of Coach's hand-me-downs.
I bolt up nineteen flights.
No one's home.
It's too quiet,
and something's not right
in my room.
Everything's slightly out
of place,
askew.
Someone's been in here.
My heart stops.
That could never happen,
not with my money.
This is the only money
I have.
Besides, I hid it—
and who steals from a kid
anyway?

I check the slit in my pillow,
and find white stuffing on the floor,
on the bed.

Nothing.

Empty.

Gone.

Ten times feeding the tabby,
The last time, Mom found the key
and went in there late at night,
and after that, Mrs. Johnson stopped asking me

to feed her cat Ollie.

I tear all the white fluff out,
shred it
into a million pieces
all over my floor.
I don't like crying
because it doesn't change anything,
but I wanted those cleats so bad.
And I know I live with a monster
whose love is stoned
love. Stone love.

Some Girls

On Monday morning Ruby is waiting
outside my building.
"Great game Saturday.
Where'd you go so fast?"

I shrug. "Home."

"I stopped by."

"You did?"
I never answer the door anymore.
"I was probably sleeping."

I see Will up ahead walking his sister to school.
If I don't hurry up, I'll miss breakfast,
and I'm starving.

"Can you slow down?" Ruby says.

"Just thinking about pancakes with syrup."

"You're always starving. Here."
She hands me a Whole Foods blueberry muffin.

"You sure you don't want it?"

"Yeah. Did you get your Messis?"

I stuff half the muffin in my mouth.
"Didn't have enough money."

"What? I thought you did?"

"I thought I did too."

"Do you want to borrow some?"

"It's okay."
What am I going to say, that I need all of it?
When Ruby asked me about the tracks
on Mom's arms all those years ago,
I told her what Mom told me to tell her.
That she had to get blood drawn at the hospital.

Now Ruby asks, "Everything okay?"

"Yeah." I'm living a lie.
That's what I do.
Or lose Mom.
That's the deal.

If I were Ruby, I'd have Whole Foods muffins every day.
"Can you please get a phone? It's like impossible
to get a hold of you when I need to talk."

"Sure, I'll get one this afternoon." I smile.

Will must have jogged ahead.
He's already in the basketball court
with some girls who steal his hat.
One of them runs her hands
through his fluffy hair, laughing.
They're party girls, loud and colorful,
unlike me. It's only a matter of time
till he and everyone else see
who I really am—

white girl who doesn't know
who her father is,
whose mother is a junky.

Some girls toss Will's hat
back and forth. Ruby and I stop
and watch them for a minute.

I take my ball out of my backpack,
daydreaming I'm zigzagging
down the field, chipping one
over the goalie's head—*score*!
Then I blast it from the corner,
bending it, like, yeah, Beckham.
Top that when I scissor kick it in backwards—
score again!
Some girls on my team carry me
up high like I'm their hero.
Some girls give me money
for pizza, an Orange Crush, Messi swag—
then my dream stops short.

In the court, some girls are singing,
"Please me" like Cardi B.
"Tease me.
Lemme hear you say please—"
Will's laughing along with them.

Ruby looks at me. "You should do something
about that. That should be you
instead of them."

My heart is beating so fast
I have to press my ball to my chest
to stop it,
please.

Can't You Hear Me Knocking

After practice
I see Sugarman
coming down
the walkway.

When things are good
everyone's happy,
but when they're not
Foxface's dealer makes
Foxface look like a little lamb.
Mom's too busy howling,
scratching, and begging
to notice anything.

First time I heard
Sugarman knocking
I let him in,
and saw his red, scabbing,
lumpy, needle-marked self.
She was kicking like a spoiled thing
who would have done anything
he said when he took out his sugar,
drawing her closer.

Foxface didn't want to share Mom.
Snot was running down his cheeks
into his mouth, open enough to see
his sharp yellow teeth.
He was crying
into his beard,

making it even pointier.

I was out the door,
down nineteen floors
till my chest hurt
and I was dizzy
from so many turns
on the stairs.
I hid in the laundry room
and when I got hungry,
I opened my mouth
and ate the sweet air.
Run, run as fast as you can,
you can't catch me, Sugarman—

Before Sugarman knocks
on our door today,
I grab my ball
and get out of there
as fast as I can.
He makes me sick,
her begging makes me sicker—
I'm gone.
When I get to the lobby,
I stop. How long can I do this?
Wanna say,
What about our pact, Mom?
You and me
forever?

Gimme Shelter

I wait in the courtyard with my ball.
Cold air's blowing in,
and I feel myself going
                                                            down
                                                                        fast.

It's dark so early, and winter's coming.
Holding on by a thread to the finals.
Close my eyes and wish
I was somewhere else.
Anywhere. I hate her
                        for making me sit
                        in the cold.

When I open my eyes
Will is standing in front of me.
"Wanna kick it around, Ceti?"

            I say, "I dunno, it's kinda cold."

"What? That's a first. You okay?"

            "Sorta."

"Can I sit down?"

            "It's a free country."
            I smile sideways.

The icy air blows leaves and trash

up around us. He pushes a strand
of my long hair behind my ear.
It feels so nice my eyes fill up.
I can't look at him.
"Hey," he says softly, "let's go inside."

The early traffic whooshes by
like ocean waves breaking
and the wind presses in.
I don't move,
not even when the sleet
starts coming down at a slant.

"Come on, pretty girl." He takes my hand.
"Don't fade on me."

I look at him to make sure he's not joking,
not about the fading part—
the pretty part.

"I can't go home right now," I say.

"Come to my place then."
He rolls my ball up on his toe,
lifts it high enough to cradle
in his arm.

He doesn't let me go
as we head inside
out of the cold.

Angie

Will's mom's cooking chicken with coconut and curry.
She turns from the steam to say hi.
"How's your mother?" she asks.
She sounds like she means something more.
Like she knows why I was sitting in the courtyard before.

"Um, fine," I say.

They have a picture of Martin Luther King
framed in their living room.
We have one of the Rolling Stones.
Angie says, "She looked like she might be under the weather
when I saw her—"

"She was sick, but she's fine now,"
I say way too fast.

"Uh-huh. That's good then." Angie turns back to the stove.
"How's the soccer team going?"

"Semifinals are Wednesday."

"You let anyone else score a goal yet?"

I laugh,
feeling those dark clouds lifting.

"I started playing soccer," Nia says.

"Bet you're good," I say.

"I'll play with you sometime."

"When?"

"Whenever you want."

"Can I braid your hair?"

"Okay."
It's warm and smells so good in here,
and there's no Sugarman or Foxface,
just Nia's small fingers massaging my scalp.

"Your hair is pretty," she says.
"You know what I'm gonna be when I grow up?"

"What?" I say.

"A horseback rider."
Will snickers too loud.
"What? I am!" Nia says.

"I always wanted to ride horses," I say.
"I used to dream I was galloping so fast."
I don't say that once I thought my dreams
would come true. Or that dreams don't always last.
Sometimes they stay way in the past.

Nia tilts her face toward mine,
her dark hair brushing my cheek.

I tell her, "In fifth grade
Will wrote his dream for the year
was to eat a lot of ice cream."

She giggles. "That figures."

Will goes, "How do you know that?
You weren't even in my class."

        "I saw it on the bulletin board."
        Truth is, I remember every single thing
        about him.

"Will, set the table for me. Your father will be home
any minute and I've got to work tonight."

"There's my dream." He sighs.

        "I should go," I say, walking to the door.

Will follows and whispers in my ear,
"Hey, don't look so sad. You're not going far."

        He has no idea.

"Life is good, okay?"

His mom is watching us.
She lowers her eyes.

Will steps outside the door.
His lips graze
my cheek, my hair.
"Come back and watch a movie with me
this weekend?"

        "Okay." I can barely breathe.

I get in the elevator, but I go down instead of up.

I wait outside till Sugarman finally rolls on out—
saccharine sweet.

How
do I keep
my dreams

up

from going

in smoke?

Miss You

Sugarman's gone,
Mom's door is closed
and Foxface is alone
on the couch except for empty bottles,
Walking Dead playing cards, and cigarettes.

"Where's she?" I whisper.

"Sleeping. Keep your freakin' voice down."
He starts dealing.
Eyes are red and puffy.
"Play War with me."

"One game. I have homework,"
I say.

"You gettin As?"

"Math and gym," I say carefully.
I flip my card. We both have eights.
"War."

Three cards down then flip again.
Mine. I sweep them toward me.

"I got an A in fourth grade," he says.

I smile a little, afraid to ask
if that was his one and only.

"What's so funny about that?
No one gave a flying—"
Card smacks down.
"War! This one's mine."
His gold cross earring shines
in the light.

"Hell, double war!" He smiles all wide
and goofy, which throws me off.
He wins this one.

            Then Mom groans—
and I start to get up, but he stops me,
his tattooed skull knuckles too close
to my face. He throws his cards down.
Leans forward,
his fox folding
into the skull.
He's so close
I can smell the smoke
and beer on his breath.
"I know she asked you
to get high. Don't worry,"
he says, lips thinning,
curling in. "I won't let her.
I'd never waste it

on you."

You Can't Always Get What You Want

Next day at lunch
Will and his basketball buddies
go to the court to shoot.
Season's changing.
Their groupies follow.

"I went to his house yesterday,"
I tell Ruby.

She squints.
"Then why isn't he hanging out with you right now?"

I shrug.
"Don't think his mom's exactly
crazy for me."

"Why not?"

"Dunno. She expects someone better?"

"Come on, we're going over there."

"No."

Ruby pulls me outside.
We lean against the brick
at the edge of the court.
The blast of November wind
isn't as cold as his groupies.

"Lookie," they say, "it's Will's *little sister*."

Ruby goes, "What's that supposed to mean?"

"That's so sweet," another one goes.

The skinny one steps up to me.
"It means his little sister—"
She points in my face.
"The wrong color
and in the wrong place."
They all laugh.

I flinch, sway back,
feel the heat spread over my face.
Getting so good at stuffing the hurt away.

Will keeps shooting.
I close my eyes
to block out their laughing
and his swishing.
Girls run onto the court, steal his ball,
and dribble right up against him
pressing close.

Ruby goes, "Annoying sophomores."

Will doesn't seem to mind, he's smiling,
playing along. Tyler joins in.
They're grinding up against him too,
eyes on us.

"Seriously?" Ruby looks at me.
"What happened yesterday anyway?"

"Nothing, I guess," I say.
"He was probably just being nice
or something. Can we go now?"

"Hey, Will," Ruby yells. "Come on over here."
He doesn't even look up.

One of the girls goes, "Keep away!"
Throws it to the skinny one, her braids flying.
"You cover Tyler, I got Will."
Her skinny arms are all over him.
Someone starts up Drake.
"Turn his lame ass off—"
one of them says.

"Let's go." I start to turn.

"Will, I know you hear me."
They all keep laughing and grinding,
saying nothing.
Ruby does though.
"Hey, Will,
you know what Martin Luther King said?"

Basketball bounces back at us.

Ruby fires out, "He said, 'Silence is betrayal,'
my friend. Shoot that into the hoop!"

"Yeah, *shoot that into the hoop*!"
the girls yell back.
"Say bye to your little sister, Will—
doesn't the soccer star play basketball?"

Ruby snatches my arm

just as the bell rings
and yanks me back inside.
"Number one rule," she says,
"if you can't get what you want,
then you get what you need,
which is definitely not this."

Ruby Tuesday

Ruby's usually swinging
her hips side to side as she walks,
like she owns the sidewalk,
and everyone else is just clearing a path for her.
I used to wish I was half white and half black like her
cuz she's so pretty and she's got a place
wherever she goes.
Only place I feel right
is on the soccer field.
Ruby says you got to use what you got,
but when I walk like that and throw
my hair back like she does
I just look like an idiot.

Today Ruby's not taking long, certain steps.
"I have to tell you something," she says.
"I wanted to tell you before.
I should have told you,
but I didn't think I'd get in,
and I didn't think they'd make me go."
She stops and turns to me.
"I'm gonna transfer to that school, you know—"
She looks down. "The private school."

As soon as she says *private,*
I feel her slipping away.
I can see her new rich friends
wearing the right thing,
saying the right thing,
going to the right places.

They'll ski on the weekends in the winter
and go to sleepaway camp in the summer.

"Why do you have to go?"
My stomach turns
over,
lurching
like crazy.
All I can think
is: *what am I*
gonna do?
She's been my best friend
for so long.

"My dad really wants me to."

"You can't."

"It's not like I'm moving or anything.
I'll be right here."

"Right." I swallow dry air,
my breaths quick and shallow.
That song Will plays,
"I Fall Apart," starts up in my head.
That's me,
small stabs in my chest
like I'm drowning.

Have You Seen Your Mother, Baby?

At home, I find one of Mom's friends
strung out on our couch,
dark straggle of hair hanging
over a red-splotched, pasty face,
eyes half closed,
looking through Foxface's *Walking Dead* cards.
Seriously, Mom and her friends
should audition for the freaking show.
She finally sees me standing there.
"What are you doing here?"

"I live here."

"Have you seen your mother?" junkie says,
waaaaaaayyyyy spaced out.

Something's burning.
"Mom!" I scream
and follow the smoke straight to her bedroom.
She's holding a burning yellow paper,
ashes floating from the fire.
Mom's eyes flash at me.
They're on fire too—wild and red.
She screams when the fire
reaches her hands.
I grab her bedspread and smother her,
so she falls back,
floating black ash
sticking to her singed hair.

Eyebrows look rubbed off,
eyelashes only stubs.
"Help me, Ceti—
I'm burning for crissake!"

I run to get cold water
and find Mom's junkie friend
in my room, looking through my stuff.
She sneers, hiding her hands.

"This is my room!" I yell,
and yank her like a ragdoll,
pushing her into the hall
before I bolt the door.

Run a pot of cold water to her room.
Mom's laughing on the bed like it's a big joke
that she almost burned us
down.
Smoke alarms were pulled out a long time ago.

She plunges her hands
in the pot, laughing
harder.

"You could have killed us!" I say.

She keeps on laughing till she's choking.
"Babe, I can't die—if I'm already dead—"

A corner of paper on the floor reads
"Roosev"—and the Os are soccer balls.
Only one person I know does that.
I snatch it up.
"This is from Gramps? He wrote—"

Then I know.
Press the paper into my palm.
Swallow.
How many?

She keeps laughing.

"You said he moved.
He wasn't at Roosevelt anymore.
You said he never wrote back to me—"

She throws up her arms.
"I don't know where he is.
He never gave me a goddamn anything.
Nothing."

My throat is stuck—
nothing comes out.

"It's an old letter, Ceti.
What's it matter?"

"Mom!" I scream.
"It matters! Does he have a number?
Do you know anything?
I need to know."

Her phone starts ringing like he heard me
or something.
Mom glances down,
then stands straight, pushes her hair back,
frowns, and clears her throat.
"Hello?
"Yes," she answers in a deep voice.
"I can start tomorrow morning."

Pause.
"I'll be there early. Thank you."
Then she throws her phone
across the room and yells,
"I got a job! I should make fifty a day easy.
We're gonna be back in the money."
She snaps her fingers.

"What about Gramps?
Do you know where he is?"

"I haven't heard from him in years."
She runs into the bathroom,
combs her hair, puts on foundation
eyeliner, and lipstick.
"Let's celebrate," she says.
She takes my hands
in her burned red fingers,
and pulls me close.
"We're starting over.
Come on, Ceti,
dance with me."
She swivels and spins her skinny hips,
flips her hair back. "Like we used to, Ceti,
you know, when we danced like Jagger."

My arms and legs are so heavy
it's like I'm shifting lead
right to left.
She can't see
that I'm not here—
that I feel *nothing*
but a smoldering
hate.

But Gramps wrote me a letter—
even if he didn't get my letters
he wrote to me.
Is he still at Roosevelt?
I should have mailed those letters myself—
I will. Tomorrow.
I'll write to him as soon as Mom lets me go.
How long will this job last anyway?
And do they know that she has no
eyebrows?

Send It to Me

Dear Gramps,

I miss you so much.
Do you know sometimes I can see you
in the crack of light beneath my door.
Are you still at Roosevelt Towers?
Will you come to watch me play soccer?
I want to tell you everything.
I didn't know you wrote—
I never got your letters or anything.
Send it to me at this return address at school ONLY.
Please please please get this, and please please write back.

Love,
Ceti

Rocks Off

Mom and Foxface are guzzling
from a bottle of something bubbly.
They're up late, partying
while I try to do my geometry.

Can't sleep, can't sleep, can't sleep—
Keep seeing the house burning.
Next morning I'm so tired
all I want to do is keep on sleeping,
dreaming about being in Florida
with Mom and Ruby, palm trees swaying
in the breeze. We're swimming
in the sea, the air warm and salty.

Outside it's gray-white November.
I want the night back, not day.
Just as I'm closing my eyes again
to get back to the blue heat, the sea air,
Foxface yells, "Get your friggin' rocks off
some other time! Your skinny ass
is gonna be fired before you start."

She's crying,
coming down
hard
again,
saying, "I can't do it.
I can't.
I'll go tomorrow.
I'm sorry."

If something happens to Mom

where would I go?
Not with Foxface.
To Gram's in Florida?
I don't think so.

Salt of the Earth

We went to Gram's once. I have the picture.
The water was dreamy blue,
not like the murky gray of the pool
that leaves you stinking like chemicals.
Only thing was, Gram didn't actually want us at all.
We got in her space at home and we didn't fit in at church.

I asked her, "Do we have to go to church every day?"

"These people are the salt of the Earth, young lady.
You should be saying your prayers too."

At least till five sharp when it was cocktail hour.

Mom had enough praying too.
She woke me early on the fourth day
and we took off in Gram's old Chevrolet.
From outside Disney, we saw the magic castle so high
and the water park, Peter Pan, Treasure Island—
we smelled roasted chicken and fries.
My stomach hurt I was so hungry
for one of those giant legs of dark meat
Mom showed me in the pictures.
We stood outside our car in the parking lot,
Mom in her jean shorts and bikini top
with a sign that said "Need Ticket."
Lots of men walking in with their families
looked at her and smiled, but no one gave us money
for a ticket.

After a while, Mom said,
"I've heard the lines are so bad
that you're waiting half the day.
Anyway, they all look like zombies."

    I said, "Salt of the earth zombies."
    And we laughed.

"Come on, we're gonna make it real," she said.
"Rich people are assholes anyway."

We got in Gram's car and took off.
First, we stopped at Store 24 and loaded up
on potato chips, cheese curls, Orange Crush for me
and cold beer for Mom, and then we headed to the beach.
We put on sunglasses and hats, spread a big towel out,
and played What-Would-You-Do-With-A-Million-Dollars-
If-You-Had-It.
We made sand castles and swam in the waves,
and after, the salt coated our skin.
When we licked our arms,
the white disappeared like magic.

I remember when the sun
started going down,
pink and orange ribbons
painted the sky like a river
floating into the sea.
I think it was the best day ever.
I want to go back
now—

just
don't
know
how.

Let It Bleed

It hits me all at once—
semifinals are today.
I leave Florida behind,
get dressed, grab my backpack,
        call out, "Bye, Mom!"

Nothing.

Foxface slams the door.
He was supposed to give Mom a ride.

        "Mom, semifinals are today,
        you know?"

Nothing.

        "Mom?"

Nothing

        "Mom!"

I open the door.
Her arm is red, hanging
over the side
of the bed,
blood streaming
from her veins
down to her hand, dripping
off her fingertips onto the rug.

I run to get paper towels or napkins—
there's only a dirty kitchen rag
and I need something clean.
I unroll the last of the toilet paper
I stole from school,
run it under the faucet,
making a pool of water.
I press the wad
to her skin,
but the blood keeps
coming.

"Mom, please stop now—"

"My damn veins are too small that's all, honey."

I sprint to my room, take a T-shirt,
wrap it around her arm, pull it tight,
press my thumb down hard.
Count *one two three four five*—

When the blood finally stops,
I lean against her, rest my head
on her shoulder,
and whisper,
"I had a dream we were in Florida.
We were swimming and the water was so blue.
Can we go back?" I swallow.
"Just me and you?"

"Okay," she says, "but we can't stay with Gram."

"We can stay somewhere else."

I lean closer.

She has a new skull tattoo behind her ear,
tiny and dark.
Like a little death.

"Lie down with me.
Come with me. Please, Ceti,"
she says, pulling me in.
"I'm so alone—"

> "Mom, I have to go—
> my game, it's today—"

"Oh right, the big soccer star.
I almost forgot we have a star in the house.
Stupid me." Her laughter
cuts straight through me.
She keeps laughing, rolling away from me.
"She's going to be someone.
Even though her mother's
a freakin' no one."

> "You're someone, Mom—"

"Babe, don't take my head.
Don't play with me," she says.
"And good luck today,
soccer star!"

> "I gotta go—"
> I back away from her.

"Just go, Ceti.
I mean,
Messi—"

Her laughter follows me
as I run out the door.

Citadel

Nationals
mean
nothing—
not a dream
but a joke.
Why did I think
I could be someone?
Maybe play for the U.S. team.
I'm nothing.
Not a star, a no one.
Nobody.
That was only a story
I told myself.

Once upon a time
it was just me and her.
She said, "We're starting over,"
and we came here
with our clothes and CDs
and called this place our citadel,
our palace in the sky.
It *was* for a little while.

Seems to me
we've been starting over
forever,
me and Mom.
Everyone else's mom
seems so normal
compared to mine.

I add her to the top of my X-list:
Mom
Ruby
Will.

When the elevator door opens
I run into the gray,
looking back once
at our citadel.
Our cement high-rise
looks like a jail.

Backstreet Girl

Will's got new red Jordans,
same ones as Kaya, who's laughing
and singing, walking too close
to him, heading toward me.
Her hair is piled high
like a crown, her jeans too tight.
She frowns at me down the hall.
I slow my step, fall back.
                That should be me.
If I had a phone, Will could text me
about the movie we're supposed to see
this weekend. He nods when he passes.
I don't want his sympathy.
I don't need to be at the bottom
of anyone's list, like some stupid little sister.
Bet his mom said to stay far away from me
cuz my mom's a junkie.
And yeah, I guess she's right.
I'd stay away from me too.
My mom doesn't even want me
around today.

I keep walking, even when he turns
and goes, "Good luck today."
He can keep that to himself.
I'll just keep myself
to myself.

Tumbling Dice

In study hall, last period before the game,
I hear about the swastikas and racial slurs
in the girls' and boys' bathrooms,
about the graffiti on the walls and mirrors,
they say cuz Trump won the election.
Joyce announces she's going to organize a protest.
Puts her bag and iPhone down on the table,
and marches off to the principal's office.
Ka-ching!

I know what I'm gonna do.
Gotta take a chance.
What do I have to lose?
What does it matter?

Might fix what's wrong
                    with me and Mom.

All I have to do is slip the phone
into my pocket. No one will know.
Anyway, Joyce probably has insurance,
or her parents will get her another one.
I put my backpack down,
slide my hand over her phone
lift my pack back on,
and get out of there
like I'm walking
                    on fire,

telling myself I'm doing it
for Mom.
                    Liar.

Jigsaw Puzzle

Foxface is making his famous
jelly and bacon sandwich
with cheese and ketchup
and whatever else is in the fridge.
"Hey, girl," he says and carries his plate
to the porch. "Did you win your game?"

"It's at 6. Bus leaves at 4:15."

He nods, spitting as he chews.
"You have any more?"

"Finals are Saturday."

"You mean, if you win today."

"We'll win."

Orange fox on his neck goes up and down
like it's chomping his sandwich too.
"Maybe I'll come see the soccer star."

"Will she come too?"
I nod toward her room.

Ketchup squeezes out of Foxface's mouth.
Lips curve into a sort of smile
and he wipes his face on his T-shirt.
Lifts his MAGA cap,
then pushes it down. "Maybe."

The road looks like a gray snake below,
winding away from here.

"I got something."
As soon as I say it,
I wish I didn't.
Last thing I wanna do
is make Foxface proud.

"What?"

"New iPhone."

"Nice." He licks his lips. "Lemme see."
His eyes shift and slant, and he shows his teeth.

"I hid it at school," I lie.
"I'll go get it."
I fly out the door
before he can stop me.

"Hey, get back here!"

I'm already gone.
I find a grassy patch away from the road.
A dude with dreads paces, blowing smoke,
crazy woman rattles her bottles—
all of us hiding back here
like we don't belong anywhere.
Drizzle on my face feels so good.
My head is scrambled,
like a puzzle I can't put back
together.

All these lies and excuses to keep her
where she is.

Don't want this phone anymore—
Joyce has always been nice
to me.
That's one piece.
Another one is Gramps.
And where Ruby used to
be.

Will is a piece,
whatever that means.

And stupid Foxface.

The darkest piece

is Mom's arm bleeding all day—

and I am
a
falling
star—not a soccer star,
not a soccer star, not a soccer star, not a soccer star.
I can't change anything.
The scout is supposed to come this Saturday.
Drizzle turns to rain.
Doesn't matter.
Who cares.
I'm nothing.
Nobody.

This phone

is about to get rained on. I hide it
between
my books.

It won't change anything between
me and Mom, won't change
all the messed - up
pieces.

It won't make me
have Mom back,
Ruby stay,
Will
or Gramps—
wherever he is.

I'm losing

myself—

can't breathe right.

The first time I saw Mom knot a strip of rubber
around her arm
and push a needle under her skin
and blood drip out,
I couldn't breathe.

I was trying to
and I couldn't.
I ran down the stairs.
Couldn't breathe,
couldn't talk.

Then Will said my name,

put his hand on my back,
and I gulped the air.

Too many pieces.
I could take the easy
way out—and go with Mom—
where she is—out there—
away from here—
fly away
and never
come back.

Rain

falls

and

falls,

and

keeps

falling

until

I

can't

tell

rain

from

tears

from

rain.

The last time with Gramps,
we played soccer till the sky was dark.
He said, "We'll come back to the park
tomorrow. Ceti girl, you could play
in the World Cup one day.
You know that, right?"

I didn't say anything.

"Ceti?"

Nothing.

"I only got one best girl, and she's going to be someone.
She already is. How much, Ceti girl?"

"More than all the stars," I said.

"Count them," he said.

I laughed. "You can barely see the stars,
Gramps."

"They're there," he said. "You know,
you can only really see the stars when it's dark enough."

Yeah, I know he can't hear me now,

but I say it anyway,
so softly
it's barely a sound,
"Hey, Gramps,
it's dark
enough now,
it's so dark,
Gramps.
Can you hear me?"

He's been so far away,
but now he feels close.
I know it.
I don't know if soccer's gonna save me
anymore, but I do know if I give up now,
I lose my dream
and everything good—

and I know I gotta breathe,
breath by breath,
piece by piece,
or I'm nothing.

Someone calls Joyce's phone
and chimes ring out
like music in the wind.
The guy with the dreads
turns and heads my way
like I'm calling him.

Got to go.
Don't know
anything else,
except I got a game
to play.

She Smiled Sweetly

On the way back to school
I go over all the excuses Mom gave me
over the years. She smiled and said,
"Babe, I think he up and married
the lady he was sweet on in his building.
Or he just left Roosevelt Towers
without a forwarding address.
Who knows, babe, maybe he's senile.
Or he's got a new best girl." *Ha ha ha*
"Besides," she said, "he could visit us.
It's not like he doesn't have our address.
Why should we go back there?
He's not that old.
Maybe his freakin' flip phone finally died."
Blah, blah, blah
Ha ha ha

Why do grown-ups tell us we gotta tell
THE TRUTH
when they don't? Instead we get lies, lies, and more lies.

Our school secretary, Mrs. Wheeler,
who has dyed blonde hair, wears crazy high heels
and bright red lipstick, doesn't lie.
She buzzes me in and hands me a cookie.
Then asks how Mom is doing like she already knows.
My world is becoming the people who know,
and those who don't. "How are things, Ceti?"
She rubs lotion on her skin.
"Ready for the big game?"

“Yeah, I guess,” I say.
“Um, I found this phone.
I think I must have grabbed it
by accident with my backpack
when I was leaving today.
I didn’t mean to—”

“I know.” Her office clock ticks.
“Joyce’s parents called. They tracked it.”
She smiles sweetly.

Now what?

I put the phone on her desk
and turn to go.

“Good luck,”
Mrs. Wheeler calls out.

I Just Want to See His Face

When I get to the school bus, Coach tells me,
"Start breaking these in, Ceti."
She hands me an Adidas shoebox.
I'm shaking so bad, my fingers fumble and lock.
Inside are the cleats I wanted—shock blue
with darker blue jags, three silver stripes, and blue laces.
They glow in the sun, look like they're racing
before I put them on. And no more slouch socks
for me—these are new and whitest white.
"Thank you," I say, hiding my face
so she can't see my wet eyes.

"You earned those, Ceti," she says,
but I don't believe her.
I hear
Just go, Ceti,
I mean Messi—

Coach must not know
about Joyce's phone.

I slide the new socks on and cleats.
They fit perfectly.

We're playing under the lights
tonight. The fluorescent glow shines
through the dark clouds,
and I think of Messi
looking up to the sky before he plays,
and I know now why he does that.

He believes in someone higher
than himself—
someone even better.
I want to believe in someone like that.
Gramps prayed sometimes. He'd kneel,
hands clasped, and his face all quiet.
When I asked why he was praying,
he'd say, "For you to get five goals today.
At least."
He smiled so big, his silver teeth flashed.
"Shhh, don't tell anyone. I got connections."
He pointed to a picture of Jesus on the wall.

It's not like I want to walk around talking
about Jesus, I just wanna see his face.
Want to know that he's looking at me today,
believing in me even when I can't.
I tighten my laces—cleats feel so good
as I jog around the field.

Hear them talking, saying,
That's the one. Watch her. Double-team her,
shut her down, keep her from scoring.
We could trip her right now. Ha ha ha.

Night clouds are crossing the sky fast.
I see a crack, looks like a smile—
maybe that's what Messi sees.
Maybe that's Jesus's face.
I look into the black,
feel myself filling up—
and something
feathery cool
lifts me—
something like hope.

Connection

Messi said,
"You can overcome
anything,
if and only if
you love something
enough."

I pass back for a give-and-go,
sprint down the line, left then right,
fake out. I'm on fire,
flying down the field—
bang it across the middle.
It curves into the corner—*score*!
Then I head one over the goalie,
send another one through
the defense for a breakaway.
Messi cleats are soaring high—
they got a connection.
We win three to zero.

It's when I get home
that everything starts going
in the wrong direction.

Mom notices my cleats right away.
"Where'd you get those, babe?"

"Coach gave them to me."

She nods, her face a mask.

"School just called.
Said you took Joyce someone's phone.
Sure you didn't trade the phone in for those?"

I look down.
Foxface's Bananagram tiles are spread
out on the table, spelling the words
WEED, TIGER, BUT.

"I guess you can't play
in the finals after all."

"WHAT?"
My head pounds.
Stomach turns.

She shrugs. "Some stupid school rules.
Sorry, shooting star."

I can't tell what she means anymore.
Can't tell if she's high or in between.

"There'll be other games."

Not this year. Can't
feel myself, can't
move. Numb. My mouth
isn't working either.
I brought the phone
back. *Noooooooooooooooooooooooooo—*

"Next time, don't get caught."

What about the scout?
I need to get back

to where I was—gotta
find that connection,
that hope
to lift me up
again.

Let's Spend the Night Together

Mom fills a pot with water
and puts it on the stove,
throws in spaghetti.
"Hey, let's hang out,
you know, like we used to."

Can't play in the finals Saturday,
can't play, can't play, can't play, can't play—

"Don't let me down, Ceti.
Take off your backpack
and stay a while.
Spend the night!"
She swipes Foxface's Bananagram tiles
off the table, on to the floor
so they scatter everywhere.
Laughs high and crazy
as she puts down two plates.
"You only live once, right?
Come on, let's get the sauce going."

Can't play, can't play, can't play—
I got to hold on to something.

"Ceti, I'm sorry about this morning.
I'm gonna clean up my act.
I went to the clinic today."

"You did?"

"Yeah, I did."
She smiles, her watery green eyes
full of something I felt when the sky
opened and smiled down on me.

Hope.

Do I dare say it?

Hope.

I don't know what's real

Her laughing turns to crying
and then back to laughing
like she can't tell the difference
anymore. "I got us some rolls,
and butter, or I got us some butter
to go with our rolls."
She opens the oven—
smells like a home.

Hope.

I kick Foxface's tiles
like I'm going for a goal—
and she laughs harder.
"Tonight, we're a team,
Ceti, you and me.
That little bastard can go straight to—
Score!"
She high-fives me as a tile
goes skidding under the stove.

All I ever wanted was to be on her team.

If Foxface is gone and Mom's getting clean—

Hope.

"Go ahead, try to score on me,"
she says, standing in the doorway between
the kitchen and living room,
waving her arms, like that's what goalies do,
right?

I wind up and kick as many tiles
as I can through her legs,
bouncing them off the walls,
refrigerator, and cabinets.
"What do you know,
an A, S, S, H, O, L—" she says.
"Now try to play your stupid
Bananagrams!"
We're both laughing so hard

something
breaks
inside me.

Hope.

The spaghetti boils over
and we laugh harder.
It's good Foxface
isn't here now.

Hope.

Maybe they called Mom
before they knew

I returned Joyce's phone.
We sit down for supper.
Smells like I remember it.

Hope.

Moonlight Mile

Mom's next to me
in my bed.
She looks younger
when she's sleeping—
her lips open, a smudge of sauce
on her chin.
Her cheeks don't look
as hollowed out,
but she's still got
lines around her eyes
and gray streaks in her honey hair.
She told me noses and ears
never stop growing,
but hers are the perfect size.
Her ears are like flower petals
and her nose is pierced
with a tiny diamond.
I stare at her for so long
her face starts to look crazy.
In the dark it's all hazy,
like I'm looking through a window
at her,
            rolling away
so her hair hangs down
like a curtain,
like she's hiding her dreams
            miles away.
I want her to say,
Ceti, I'm coming home now.
Here I am. I'm home now

to stay.
Flakes of snow swirl outside,
falling from the moon.
Every second is an hour,
remembering Mom and me
like it used to be.
It's so quiet, except for the wind
and snow blowing against the window.
And the moon keeps shining
its light down on us.
Warm air kicks in from the heater.
She must hear it rattling
cuz she opens her eyes
and says, "Come closer,
Ceti, lie
next to me."
In the dark, it's easier to ask,
"What'd they say at the clinic,
Mom?"
A siren sounds down
the road. She smiles at me,
rests her hand on her stomach.
"Guess what?" she whispers.
"You're gonna havc a baby sister,
Ceti. I got you a new sister."
Something sparks in the ashes
inside of me.
Seems like the moon
is shining a mile-long light
right through me.

Monkey Man

Throat's so dry I'm choking
on my breath.
Got to get a drink.
My brain is buzzing: a *sister*—
will she be all right?

I'm so stiff I can barely walk.
Foxface is at the kitchen table—
didn't hear him come in.
He's rearranging
his Bananagram tiles.
He asks, "Did you touch these?"

"No." I fill a cup
with water and drink
till it's empty.

"Shit, I had so many shittin'
good words. Was it her?"

"I didn't see."

His hands are fists
and his arms hang down.
He scratches and screeches
like a chimpanzee.
Takes a beer out of the fridge
and drinks it in one gulp—
buuuuurrrrpppp—
then wipes his mouth

with the back of his hand.

I start back to bed.

“What happened to the iPhone?”

“I got caught.”
Push it down. Hold it all inside.

“Nice one. Better not be any follow-up here.”

“No. No one will come here.
I’m tired, I—”

“Help me first.”
He takes a fork to scratch his back,
arches toward me, his eyes like cracked eggs,
yolks running.

I spell LEMON.

“Yeah, LEMON freakin’
squeezer, right?”
He squints, eyes all pupil,
fox snarling. “Why’d she sleep—”
He points. “In there?”

“She didn’t think you were coming back
tonight,” I say slowly, wishing for that kinda luck.

He tosses peanuts up one at a time, catches them in his mouth.
Crunch, crunch.

My legs go wobbly, shoulders collapse.
What if my new sister is a little Foxface?
Rewind. Erase.

Sway

Moon's covered by clouds
and I'm so tired I can't sleep.
My mind's playing tricks on me
in the dark.
Yellow demon eyes
watching me.
I'm not stupid,
I know what
drugs can do
to babies.

I wonder if Mom's
taking vitamins.
She said that's why
I did everything early.
She said I ran
before I walked,
and I was kicking
a ball when I was one.
I'll teach my sister
to play soccer.
I'll get vitamins
for Mom
so my sister's strong—
I have to take care of her,
I'm the one.

Can see my baby sister now,
smiling from the corner
of my room, swaying
me
to a better place.

Rip This Joint

"Gotta make some runs,
babe, get dressed."
Foxface lights a joint
on the porch, sucks it in,
swallowing the smoke.
Passes it to her.

"No!" I start to say.
"My sis—"

"Go to school, Ceti,"
Mom says in her tiny pink
underwear and T-shirt.

"Where were you last night?"
He blows out.

Hand on her hip, Mom pouts
and points to my room.

"Come on, we gotta go.
We got some visits to pay.
Get your starter started."
With one hand, he pinches her butt
and with the other grabs his MAGA hat.
"And look half decent."

Bruises run up and down
her long arms and legs
like tattoos. She says,

"New Hampshire today,
babe?"

He waves her away
in a cloud of smoke.
"Come on, got to rip."
Snap, snap.

In her room, I say bye to Mom
and then to my sister.
Put my mouth on her belly
and *kiiisssss* her.

"Shhhh," Mom says.
"He doesn't know yet."

My heart beats so fast
I think it's going to blast
right through my chest.

Dead Flowers

"What are you two whispering about
in there?" Foxface says.

Mom picks up a drooping bouquet
of pink carnations. "These for me?"
He snorts, and I bolt out the door.

She told *me* about my sister,
not Foxface—*I* know and he doesn't.
I'm going to take care of Mom *and* her,
not him. She's *my* little sister.
But the whole way to school,
all I see are dead flowers
along the sidewalk,
in pots on doorsteps,
hanging from porches.
And I hear
everyone at school talking
inside my head:
Ceti did it. She stole Joyce's phone.
Mom's a junkie. Probably made her do it.
Now she can't play in the finals—
White trash. Loser—

If I can't play Saturday,
what am I gonna do?
Wait till next year?
Maybe that scout will come back—
along with Ruby and Will, right?
I'm so tired, I sway side to side—

want out
can't deal
don't wanna
can't stop,
swirling gray
what am I gonna do
dead flowers
what about someday
ache all over
bell rings
stop please—

All I know is I have to take care of my sister—
but I'm scared.

In the morning light
white dew shines
in the grassy weeds
like diamond beads.

Step forward,
then back.
And forward
again.

Out of Time

So tired—
          my eyes are clouds
floating over the sidewalk,
like I'm looking down on myself.
I'm a ghost, a shadow,
a nothing
as cars swoosh by.

I see school up ahead,
and I don't want to go.
I could turn around now
and go anywhere
but here—
somewhere.

What if my coach and team
turn on me—
wanna stop the voices.
Alone alone alone alone—
          weighing
          my options.

Ruby has her stupid school visit day.
Will's probably shooting hoops
and not talking
to me.
I'm
running
out
of

time.
Missed breakfast
cuz I can't
make myself
step
forward—

The sun is a white disc in the sky,
burning so bright my eyes hurt. I stall.

Then look up, and remember
the washed-out words on my soccer ball.
I have a dream—
even if it's crazy—
it's still mine,
and no one can take
that away from me.
And I have
a sister
who needs me.

One step
toward school,
then another.
Keep walking
cuz I'm more scared
of what could
happen
if I don't.

Waiting on a Friend

Soon as I walk inside, I get,
"Hey, Ceti, are you playing in the finals?
What's up with that?"

"Dunno." I shrug.

"You have to play.
They'll lose without you."

"Maybe, maybe not."

"Nice one, Ceti.
Need a phone much?"

"It was an accident."

"Joyce got her phone back,
so you're off the hook."

"What?"

"Heard she was pretty upset."

"Yeah."
My head's spinning
and I'm so hungry
my stomach's howling.
The socks Coach gave me
yesterday are dirty.
I sleepwalk down the hall.

Stop.

Nurse Emi said
I could come by to see
her any time I needed
anything.
She's soft and warm
and smells like flowers.
"Hi, Ceti," she says. "Everything all right?"

My knees are shaking.
What if she starts asking questions?

> "Um, I was wondering if you have any vitamins.
> I need some."

She opens a desk drawer
and pulls out a teddy bear bottle
of yellow, orange, and red gummies.
Pours a few in a small cup.
"I can't give you more than this,
but you can come back every day
if you need."

> I suck in air.
> "Thank you."

Nurse Emi smiles. "Of course.
You have a big game coming up."

> Something catches in my mouth—
> *the game*—I try to swallow it down.

"What is it, honey?"

I'm so tired, my face is melting

off,

so I sit down to hold it on.

Nurse Emi shuts the door to the hallway,
sits next to me on the cot, waiting.

I tell her almost all of it
(except about Mom and Foxface,
and my new sister)—
how I know I made a mistake—
I don't need to announce it
to the whole world.

Emi tells me to rest and pulls
the curtain around me.
I close my eyes and breathe in
her lavender smell.
"Maybe you should talk to Joyce later,"
she says as blackness falls
all around me like a shade.

No Use in Crying

At lunch I find Joyce.
"I'm sorry about your phone.
I didn't mean to take it."

Joyce's eyes are like taffy
pulling side to side
like she doesn't know
if she should believe me or not.
She wears a Not My President
button with a picture of Trump
crossed out.
She flicks her ponytail back.
"Thanks for returning it.
I have to pay like eighty a month.
No insurance, you know."

"Ouch," I say.
I was wrong.

"First world problem, right?"
Her eyes focus on my dirt-streaked socks.
"You know you have to play
in the finals, right?"

"What?"

"You have to play in the finals."

"Do you know if I can?"

"You brought it back, right?
It was an accident."
She smiles.

"Yeah, I did," I say,
my heart beating faster and faster.
"For real?"

She nods. "Everyone makes
mistakes. Now you better win."

Something Happened to Me Yesterday

Coach yells, "Hurry up
and get on the field with your team, Ceti,
before I make you do suicides."
She's smiling, so I don't ask questions.
I play like my life depends on it.
Girls are whispering,
"You're good. You're in.
Everything okay, Ceti?
What happened with the phone?
I heard you were sick.
You'll be there Saturday, right?"
Coach tells them, "Enough chitchatting.
Captains in front! Last one in line,
sprint to the front, twice around!"
We do, screaming, "Go Falcons!"

> Why'd Mom tell me that?
> I scream louder, "Go Falcons!"
> Why'd she say I couldn't play?

After we practice corner kicks, penalty kicks,
and headers, we gather around Coach
to go over the starting line-up for Saturday.
Hold my breath till I hear: "Striker, Ceti."
After practice they pick me up
and carry me from player to player.
And I can't help it.
I do what I said I wouldn't—
I cry

cuz I'm so happy
I belong here.

Will's hanging out on the field
after practice. "Hey, Ceti,
haven't seen you in a minute."

I go, "What's the special occasion?"

"Oh, snap, what?"

"You're talking to me."

"Right."
His hair is flying
in every direction
and I swear he's even taller
than the last time I talked to him.
Maybe his new Jordans.
"You know," he says,
"everyone's always trying
to get me to do what they want.
You don't do that."

I'm not wasting time today.
"Then why you always acting like
you don't even know me?"

"I don't—"

"Is it cuz your mom?"

"No, she likes you.
She just worries a lot.
She doesn't want me to—"

He sighs.
"She saw your mom,
um, high or something."

"Yeah, well," I say,
"I'm not my mom.
I got to go."
Got to wash my socks and uniform,
got to get these vitamins back home.
That's my news.

Torn and Frayed

"You heading back?"

I just frown and keep walking,
feeling so good I can shake off the extra.
He follows me,
          and I don't complain.

Right when we walk into the lobby,
Foxface steps out of the elevator
in his Lock Her Up shirt.
His suede coat is ripped,
frayed at the edges, stained.
His eyes are shining red, cranking.
"What's up, Ceti?" His eyes narrow.
"Who's your friend?"

          "Will.
          He lives here."

Foxface turns to Will.
"Better keep your hands off her."

Will glances at me. I roll my eyes.

"You hear me? Speak English much?"
Foxface grunts.

"What'd you say?" Will glares.

          "Let's go." I try to pull him
          away.

Will shakes me off. He's as tall as Foxface,
and bigger, all muscle, no flab.
Or blab.
He says, "Do you got something to say to me?"

"Nope, nothing." Foxface points at me.
"Better see you upstairs in five."

Will shakes his head
like he's putting it all together.
Says under his breath, "Freaking
freak."

"What was that?" Foxface says.
Then looks at me. "Ain't your heart
he wants, for your information."

Will throws his head back
and laughs. "Oh, snap,
that was good."

> I catch Will's hand, pull him
> toward the stairs. "Come on."

Will takes two, three steps at a time.
Stops, turns to me.
"Is he for real?"

> "Yeah, well, someone's gotta
> Make America Great Again.
> This is him—
> *Better keep your hands off her.*
> Foxface and Agent Orange
> are gonna save our country,

right? Those two are a match made in heaven."
I put on my stupid Foxface face—
eyes slits and mouth sharp,
everything pointed, crooked.

Will's laughter rolls through the stairwell.
Feels so good washing over me,
I'm laughing too. Can't stop.

There's a tiny hole where the button goes
in Will's corduroy jacket.
I slide my finger through it,
and he steps down beside me,
puts one hand on the side of my face.
The other pushes my hair back.
He looks in my eyes and then
his mouth is on my mouth,
his lips soft and perfect.
Everything inside of me
melts all at once.

He pulls back, whispers,
"*Ain't your heart I want.*"
And we both break up laughing
again.
Till we hear the door creak open
and footsteps pounding toward us.
Will takes my hand
and we fly
out of there.

Memory Motel

I get back before Foxface
pokes his head
through our apartment door
and gives me the up and down.
"Tell her to go to work once in a while.
She must think she lives in a motel
or something."

His zipper's undone.

"What's so funny?"

"Nothing.
I'll tell her."

"And I don't want to see you
hanging around that punk again."
Door slams.

Mom's on the porch, leaning over the railing,
her face in a cloud of smoke.
"Come here," she tells me.

I do, but I'm not telling her anything.

Without turning around, she says,
"What was he talking about?"

"Nothing. Just talking."

"He can go to hell."
She points to the road.
"Hey, there's my pick-up."
A red beat-up Ford
is cruising down the road—
like the one we used to sleep in.
Looks like a Matchbox from up here.
"Sometimes I just want
to get in something and take off.
Start all over again."
She steps on her cigarette with her toe
and kicks it off the edge of the porch.
Wind blows it out of sight.

"For real?" I say.

"Yeah." Her shoulders kinda collapse.
"I'm so tired all the time."
She closes her eyes and looks away,
her hair whipping around her face.
"He got a new job at Mickey D's,
the night shift. Seven to three."

Yesssssss!
I try not to sound too happy
when I say, "Why do you stay?"
Why is he even in the equation—
when he could be taken out?

She shrugs.
"I don't know what else to do.
Guess I'm getting old too."
She looks down.
"Don't wanna be alone."

"What about me?" I say.
"Things could be like they used to.
You know, better."

"I know, I remember, Ceti."
She looks out into the sky, black
folding into blue
into black.
"Let's eat. Can you get some mac 'n' cheese
or something at the store?"

"Come inside first, Mom."

"Don't worry, I'm not jumping tonight."
She smiles. "I'm thinking of a way out."
She gives me five crumpled dollars.
"I'll time you. Ready, set, go!"

I sprint out of there, thinking, *What if, what if, what if—*
what if she really does want to change?
Would she really leave Foxface?
Time's ticking so I race
to the Dollar Store.
Grab the mac, and notice
a bumper sticker on the rack:

JESUS LOVES YOU
(EVERYONE ELSE THINKS YOU'RE AN ASSHOLE)

Perfect for a certain someone I know,
and I got just enough dough.
Ka-ching!
Stuff it in my hoodie, and laugh my way home.
Thinking before I say goodbye to Foxface,
I'll stick this on his car and watch him drive away,

and say, "See you in some other universe, Foxface—
or not."

Mom's waiting for me in the lobby.
Says, "I'm so hungry—I can't wait.
Let's get something from the hot bar."

That's what we used to do
at Star Market. While she was *paying*,
I'd carry our food to the table—
hot wings, mashed potatoes, mac 'n' cheese, and beans.
"Okay," I say.

"I found a few more bucks around our place."
She shrugs. "Let's see what we can get."
She looks back once at the trash
someone left by the door.
"Let's blow this popsicle stand,
babe."

All Down the Line

Walking down the sidewalk,
everyone's staring at us
        like they used to. She's talking
about how she can borrow Robyn's car.
"There's a place we can go in New Hampshire, Ceti.
No one will bother us there.
Just you and me."

"Really, Mom?"

She pulls her sweater tight over her chest.
November wind blows her hair back,
showing the bruises on her neck
her make-up doesn't cover.
"Robyn knows people up there.
I could get a job. Just for a little while.
Till we come out on top."
Her eyes sparkle for the first time
in soooooo long.

"When?" I need to know.

"Tomorrow."

After the finals.
"Text Robyn then. Right now."
I suck in my breath.
If we go away, she can get clean
and then come back and be

normal?

Like *really* start over?
Can't think about whether
this will turn into another
someday.

"Just you and me?" I say.

"Yeah. I'll text her now."
She takes out her phone—
tap tap tap tap tap.

My heart fills.
I have to tell Will.

Star Market is crowded.
Mom takes a wagon, pushing it
down the aisles. Throws in
chocolate chip muffins, cherries,
cinnamon rolls, focaccia, olives,
cheese—without looking at the prices.
Humming, drumming, thrumming
all down the line. Knocks a bottle
of salad dressing on the floor,
and keeps going.
"Gotta keep the motor running."

There are cut-up apple slices for sample,
chips and salsa, cubes of cheese. We eat it all.
A woman frowns at us.
"Use a toothpick for God's sake."
Mom tells her, "Why don't you get your throttle on, lady."
The lady's mouth opens, but we don't wait around.
Mom smiles at me and I smile back.

We'll leave long enough

to lose Foxface.
Then it could be just us—
me and her, and my new sister.
I skip down the aisle.

Crazy Mama

I dig the Dixie Cup of vitamins out of my pocket.
"Here, I almost forgot."

She pops them into her mouth.
"Thanks, babe."

"Do you have any names picked out?"

"Lu-na, Luna!
You're a star, and she's the moon!
I'm making a new heaven."
She laughs and keeps pushing
our almost full wagon down the aisle.

Luna, la la la Luna!
Soon it'll be me, Mom, and Luna—I breathe in.

Mom swings her hips over to the fancy tea boxes.
I toss a milk chocolate bar into the wagon.
Look up and see Ruby waving. "Hey, you."
Ruby's mom says, "We haven't seen you for so long, Ceti.
Ready for the finals?"

"Ready as I'll ever be," I say,
praying they'll keep walking.
"We're gonna win,
I know it."

"You're amazing." She laughs.
Black suede coat, lips colored pink,

nails painted to match, white teeth,
smooth skin—Ruby's mom looks like velvet.

Mom suddenly spins toward us.
"What about me?"
She twirls around with a box of tea.

Heat scorches my face.

"Oh, I'm so sorry, I didn't recognize you,"
Ruby's mom chokes out the words.
Her eyes widen, flash white.
Her mouth tightens.
She looks Mom up and down in a second.
"It's been way too long. How are you?"

"Perfect!" Mom sings.

Ruby swallows, smiles a little.
"So nice to see you." Her voice is brittle.

"You too, honey." Mom steps closer.

Ruby looks like she's going to run.

Under the fluorescent lights,
Mom is a walking skeleton,
her cheeks sunken, red lipstick smeared,
hair oily—and she smells bad.
Not a beautiful rainbow
but a junkie mom.
Anyone can see that.

My high goes low
as fast as it takes to ditch

our shopping cart
by the bathrooms—

and bolt out of there.

Sympathy for the Devil

We don't belong in there—
we belong out here in the dark.
A cold wind whips my face.

  "Are we really going to do it, Mom?"

"Yeah, babe. Robyn said she'd drive us.
She wants what's best, you know, for us."

  "What time?"

"We have to leave by noon.
He has to make a run at eleven—"
She looks down.

  "What time'll he get home,
  Mom?"

"Right after noon." She smiles.
"Just in time to wave goodbye!"

  Game's at ten, can't tell her.
  Not after Star Market.
  They'd all know. Don't say anything—
  not till we get there.
  I've learned my lesson.
  "Good," I say. "Where?"

"I'll tell her to pick us up by your old school,
where you play soccer," she says softly.

"By noon."

Out here with Mom
everything's different.
Just me and her hiding
in the night like we used to—
before Foxface. "Mom, why him?
Why'd you do that—I mean, with him?"

She puts her hand on her chest.
"He wanted to show me *paradise*."
She opens her arms wide.
A car honks at us—we're standing
in the middle of the freaking road.
Mom flips them the bird and keeps walking.
"It made me feel good.
Like I wasn't overwhelmed anymore."
She looks at her slippers, scuffed and dirty.
"And he was sweet then."
Her voice goes soft.
"When I met him he was, you know, classy.
He made me guess his name."

I can't help but laugh.
"Classy? You mean classy
like Agent Orange classy?"

She bursts out laughing,
We can't stop. She's shaking
she's laughing so hard.
Now people are looking at us
because we're laughing, not them,
and in the dark, they can't see
the shattered tracks
that mark my mom.

"When we're in New Hampshire,
I'll tell you everything, Ceti.
Promise. We're gonna make it real.
You're my girl.
Pretty soon I'll have two girls,
but for now, you're my one and only."
I'm almost her height.
"You're so beautiful, Ceti.
That used to be me.
One night I might just sneak in
and steal that pretty face."

You're so beautiful, Ceti—
Is she talking about me?

Floating home,
the moon makes a halo
over us—me, Mom, and Luna.

I make a list:
Win the finals
Meet the scout
Talk to Will
Go to New Hampshire with Mom
Leave Foxface far behind
What about Gramps—?

"Mom, can you tell me one more thing,
please?"

"Shoot."

"Do you know where Gramps is?"
A cold breeze slaps my face.

"How about NO.
How's that for an answer?"
Her switch flips and she walks into a shadow.

"Okay, Mom. Sorry,"
I say, trying to get back
to where we were.
"We'll just make it real
like you said." I need to feel—
need to know—change is coming.

Hot Stuff

Today, Saturday, is *my* day.
Finals first, then New Hampshire.
Up early to make mac 'n' cheese

cuz there's nothing else
except Foxface's half-eaten KFC.
Grab my cleats and lucky ball
and head down.

Got to do one thing first.
He always parks his Mustang
in the same spot.

Feel like he's gonna jump out
on me when I cover his
Trump/Pence 2016
bumper sticker with the
Jesus loves you
(Everyone Else Thinks You're an Asshole) one.
Feel that scratch of laughter in the back of my throat,
swing my cleats over my shoulder
                                                            and bolt.

I'm feeling it.
Today's my day to be set free.
At the field I tighten my cleats,
warm-up with my team.
"Hey, Ceti, are you pumped?
How many goals you gonna get?
Yeah, Falcons!" High-fives all around.
Look up to the sky, not a cloud.

The blue is dazzling.
We're ready. I'm ready.
Run in place, knees up,
fists tight. Coach tells us,
"We can do this.
We're better than they are.
Work together, feed the ball outside,
then back into the middle.
Watch their striker—she's a Goliath,
and she plays the whole field."

Mean, rolling eyes,
short bleached hair, thick body,
Goliath is nothing
compared to Foxface
and Mom
when she's high.
Mom—
will be clean soon—
starting at noon today.
For now, got to get my game
on—

Whistle blows and
Goliath blows by me
and scores—
under a minute.
Look up again
to find that crack
between the clouds,
that something higher.
Cheers are like music
playing in my ears.
Music is what I want,

singing, pumping, heat rising.
No one's going to stop me.
Today I'm going to make things right.
They're chanting my name,
"Ceti, Ceti, Ceti—"

I make them all Foxface—
and they can't catch me in this race.
Dodge right, left, fake out,
pass back, give and go,
one touch up ahead.
Read the field,
two, three plays ahead,
just like Gramps said.
Don't think about leaving with Mom.
Corner kick—bolt from the eighteen—
run, run as fast as you can—
my Messis are talking to me—
bang it in with my silver toe
to tie it 1 to 1.
Goliath glares.
I'm not scared of her.
I'm running through everything—
quick touches, dodge again,
send it into space, outside, cut in—
Hear Ruby shouting from the side,
"Young, scrappy, and hungry,
I'm not throwing away my shot!"
She's here, even after last night.
Don't stop—run in and wait for it,
head down, ankles locked—
I'm *not* throwing away my shot.
Before the ball hits the grass
I boot it hard and fast.
a rocket, a missile blast—*score*!

I hear the crowd
yelling my name so loud
it lifts me into the blue.
I know what I have to do.
Game's not over,
it's only 2 to 1.
Goliath bulldozes down the field
right smack into our sweeper,
who stays down on the ground.
They carry her off and we take a knee.
"You're next," Goliath tells me.
She holds my shirt, knocks me down,
slide tackles from behind, scores.
Ref's not calling it.
Coach complains, but I'm good.
I can take it.
I jump over her.
tap it to my wing with my left.
We miss the shot,
but it's 2 to 2 at the half.
Listen to Coach and keep playing
like nothing can slow my stuff.
Tying's not good enough.
We have to win, we got this one.

But they have two, sometimes three
covering me and no one scores—
Still tied with only minutes to go.
Goliath's hanging too close
like she's been saving up.
Puts her pasty face in mine.
"Everyone knows your mother's a junkie.
Never comes to the games.
Guess you're not that good
after all."

My insides go cold—
like all the heat's been drained.
"What'd you say?"

She hisses, "I said, is your junkie mom
getting high right now?"

"No." I don't look up.
What if Foxface found out?
What if she is *getting high right now?*
Blinded, shaking, I stumble, heave,
see nothing but white—

Then the sky opens—
the light shines through
and someone smiles down on me,
telling me to believe

in me.

I hear my name—I know Coach believes in me,
and the scout is here, and Will and Ruby—
I gotta score one more.
Rage burns through me.
The ball is heading up the field—
I fly out of my stupor,
run and steal that ball,
tap it to the side, roll it back,
one-two touch, chip outside.
Then when it comes back
to the eighteen, fire it
like a bullet. It smacks
off the top corner post.
Then it's all mine,

and I won't miss
the second time.
Wind up—

then everything goes **BLACK**

like night has come
way too fast.

Worried About You

Coach says, "Don't move too fast, Ceti.
You got hit pretty hard."

    I try to sit up,
    but the world is spinning
    around
        and
    around
        and
            around.

"Go slow." She and Nurse Emi
are kneeling next to me.
"You may have a concussion."

    "No, I don't," I say.
    "I have to play—"

"Game's over, Ceti."
Her hand rests on my forehead.
"Just breathe. Yeah, that's it.
I was about to call the ambulance,
Luckily Nurse Emi was here."

    "Did we win?"
    I start to get up,
    but Nurse Emi holds me down.

"Yeah, we won." Coach smiles.
Nurse Emi says, "How'd you feel? Headache, dizzy?

We left a message for your mom.
She knows."

A scream rolls fast into my throat.
Something happened. I feel it
inside.

"I'm sure she'll—"

I put my head between my knees
I say, "You don't get it—
how long have I been out?
What time is it?"

My team surrounds me—
"Hey, Ceti, you did it!"

"*We* did it," I say.
"What time is it?"

"Yeah, Goliath got booted.
Lily got the penalty kick.
Three to two, we won the state finals!"
Their arms around me,
warm breath on my face.

I ask again, louder,
"What time is it?"

"What time is it?"
Ruby yells. "Show-time!"

Will's there too. His fingers in my hair.

Why does he make me feel like this?

Like no one else?

"You good?"

"What time is it?" Time number four.
I stand, all wobbly.
He'll get it—about getting clean,
going to New Hampshire, and making it real again.

"Like twelve fifteen."

As soon as he says it,
I see the needle sliding
under her skin,
her slumped over,
hitting the wall,
eyes floating
away from me,
and I'm
F
A
L
L
I
N
G
through a crack between

what's real what I want to be real.
what's real what I want to be real
what's real what I want to be real
what's real what I want to be real
what's real what I want to be real
what's real what I want to be real
what's real what I want to be real

"Hey, Ceti?"
Will holds my hand,
his finger on the white
lines across my palm.
A glance says it all.

I make a fist
to hide the pain.
A hammering thuds
in my brain.

"What's up, pretty girl?"
he's saying.

Unless she's waiting for me right now.

No one expects it
when I sprint away.
Will and Ruby call my name,
Coach's yelling something about the scout,
my team's telling me to come back—

but there's a chance Mom's still got my back.
I've got to get to the school field,
don't even break my stride

even if I am chasing smoke
and losing my ride—
live free
or die—
right?

Hand of Fate

I'm running crazy—
the blue sky suddenly all hazy—
got to go faster—school is empty—
Robyn, her car, and Mom aren't waiting—
my head is pounding harder—
breaths are short, heart is cracking—
Foxface will be back after noon—
don't stop
till I see
our cement box,
our home
in the clouds—
what is my fate—
dizzy and hot, crazed
and afraid I'm too late—
someone
give me a sign,
please.

Time Waits for No One

I can't turn the key
my hand's shaking so much.
          "Mom!" I call out. "Are you in there?
          Please! You said—I'm here—Mom, please—"
          I should have known—she couldn't leave.

The door finally opens.

Inside, Foxface is slumped over
all slanted on the couch,
his chin hanging on his chest,
white eyes on a gray face.

Needle, matches, and spoon
on the cushion beside him.
Orange fox is folded over,
lifeless on his neck,
and his gold cross earring
                              upside
                                        down.

          I can't breathe.
          Mom.

Bedroom is empty,
and the bathroom.
The porch—*no, Mom*—
sliding door's open,
the wind's blowing in.
She's on her back,

eyes closed, lips purple,
making a groveling sound
like she's speaking in tongues
a song that should never be sung.

"Mom, wake up. It's me, Ceti!
You have to breathe—
please, Mom—"

I pick up her hand, shake her blue fingers.
Need to call 911 now.

"Hold on, Mom," I tell her.
"Don't leave—"
Out in the hallway,
I scream,
"Someone call 911!"

Will's coming out of the elevator,
pressing numbers on his phone.

I remember
Luna
and run back,
put my ear
on Mom's belly.
Feels like a stone.
Wait for a beat, a something,

get nothing.
I tell her, "Only a little longer now.
Mom."

Will kneels on the ground beside me.
"What do we do, Ceti?

I can't remember how to do this—"

"Just try," I beg. "Do something!"

He starts pumping Mom's chest,
up and down, quick and hard.

Not real, not real, not real.

He presses into her chest again,
counting to himself. The seconds pass
like hours.

It's like a movie rewinding—
all my dreams float past
Mom's broken body
and wasted face,
passing too fast,
lost in the gray.

I say, "How much time
do we have?"
Cuz we need more
time.

WINTER

It's like winter out here
with the wind blowing
through my number 10 shirt.
I press myself close to her
till the sirens make my head hurt
          and the sky
                    bleeds red.

Two policemen arrive,
both wearing purple gloves.
White one stops at Foxface,
black one comes out on the porch.
"Found her like that?"

          "Yes."

"She your mom?"

          I nod. "Will she be okay?"

He puts his hand on her wrist.
"She's got a pulse, she's trying to breathe."
He shakes her by the shoulders till she looks like she'll snap.
That rasping sound comes out of her mouth again.
"Heroin?"

          "Yeah."

"You know how much?"

          "No. I was playing soccer."

He glances at my uniform,
eyes closing.
His partner kneels beside him.
"Death gargle."
Partner nods.
Then he holds Mom's face,
and sprays into her nose.
"Narcan deployed in her left nostril."

Wind picks up, clouds are spinning
around me, my heart is banging
around so fast and hard.
Foxface still hasn't moved.

"Come on back now, ma'am.
You got a daughter here, waiting for you,"
black cop says.
"Looks like a fine soccer player too."

"She is," white cop says.
Takes an oxygen mask
and covers Mom's face.
"Yeah, that's it. Come on now."
EMTs arrive.
Slide her on a stretcher in five.
I stand, swaying.
White cop turns to Will.
"Hold on to her for me.
Wind's picking up."

Nineteen floors up,
Will wraps his arms around me
so tight I couldn't

f

a

l

l

even if I wanted to.

Coming Down Again

It's like I'm coming down with her
as they wheel Mom out on a stretcher.
She lifts her head as they pass Foxface.
"What happened? Why's he under that blanket?
Come back to me, baby. I'm not leaving,
I'm staying with you—"
She vomits, spraying the floor,
shaking and screaming out the door.

"Sweet Jesus," Will's mother says from the doorway.
She pushes our neighbors back into the hallway.
"This isn't a carnival, folks." Then her voice goes softer,
"Ceti, honey, you can stay with us."
She knows one of the firemen.
Fragments of their talk float by me:
The kids go to school together— live in the building—
good people—

Nia takes my hand.
        That's when I lose it.
        I run to the EMT pushing Mom away.
        "What about my sister?" I cry.

He whips his head around.
"Where's your sister?"

        I touch my finger to Mom's belly.

The EMT shakes his head.
"Okay, we'll do our best,"

which means she's probably *dead.*

Luna, Luna, Luna.
I'm the star and you're the moon—

Mom screams, "It hurts!
Give me my freakin' phone!"

Outside is all gray clouds,
like the sky
is falling down
too,

except for a single bird
floating through the white.

I wish I were that bird
up so high,
sailing away
from this life.

Slipping Away

After Mom's gone, it's so quiet
it's weird. My shirt's stained with dirt,
my Messis splattered with vomit.
In the bathroom, I clean my cleats,
scrub my hands until they're red.
What if I hadn't gone to the game?
We could have left together without Foxface,
now he's dead,
and they took her away,
half-dead,
and Luna
must be dead.
Now they are only data,
numbers, statistics
to count the dead.
WHAT IF
I hadn't played soccer,
then they might not be dead.
I hear my name,
but I'm not leaving.
What's going to happen to me—
where will I go from here?
Rewind, play, rewind, fast forward.
I'm spinning backward.
Stop. Forward, again.
I thought the finals were everything,
but I was wrong.
My dream was wrong.
Just breathe,
unbreathe,

and breathe—
until they knock on the door.
Will and Ruby find me on the floor,
pick me up, one on each side.
"I'm sorry, Ceti, I didn't know till last night.
It's gonna be okay."
Ruby's crying,
like she's trying
to convince herself.

Will puts his hand under my chin.
"Say something, Ceti."

I finally look up and say,
"I could have stopped her—
We were supposed to leave today,
just me and her so she could—"

"Do you actually think you could have stopped her?
It's not your fault, Ceti," Will says.
"No possible way." He lifts my face to his.
"Look at me. Not for a second, no way,
you can't blame yourself."

"Yeah," Ruby goes, "it's a disease—
she's addicted. Now come on, please
let's get your stuff."

Now it's my turn to send
all the Bananagrams flying
off the kitchen table.
Glance over at Foxface,
covered with a blanket,
like he's gonna change
his mind about being dead,

or something.

“Hey now, okay?”
The white cop pokes his head out
of Mom’s bedroom.
“I seen you play this morning—
my daughter plays too. Izzy.”
His pale blue eyes turn milky.
“You’re a superstar.”

“I’m not.” I shake my head.

Now everyone will know.

I’m nobody.

I’m nothing

falling

through a crack,

disappearing.

Why else would she

choose this

over me?

One last look at Foxface’s *Walking Dead* cards,
then to my room. Leave the trophies behind,
pack some clothes, the picture of me and Mom,
my horse statue, one more dream
slipping away.

Outside, the sun's only a gray disk
slipping away.

Nia marches over and takes my hand
in hers, pulling me with her other hand.
"Ceti, they said you can come with us."
I bend down and she puts her face
next to mine, smiles, and says,
"You can be my sister."

Child of the Moon

White cop wipes his eyes
with his uniform sleeve.
Probably thinking about Izzy
and feeling sorry for me—
I don't need his sympathy.
His lips tighten into a smile.
"Your mom's going to come back from this."

And then what?
It happens all over
again?

"We just want what's best for you, Ceti."
The light dances off his badge.

What about
if there is no best?

"There's something else," he chokes out.
"I'm sorry, I don't think the baby—"

"I know," I say.
I see Mom moon blue,
icy cold eyes like craters,

holes

that I'm falling
through, screaming
silently,

Luuuunnnnnaaa.

Someone says, "She's in a better place."

There must be a heaven for babies
who never become babies,
who don't do anything—
don't even know
they're going to die.
There must be
a better place than here
for a child of the moon.

Dandelion

Mom's lies are blowing around inside my head—
can't hear anymore. Walk by Foxface for the last time.
Now everyone will know who I really am—
white trash junkie girl living a lie.

Will's got my ball tucked under his arm.
Ruby and Angie are in the front, clearing the way.
Holding my backpack in one hand,
Nia's hand in another, I make my feet go forward
and walk by their open doors in the hallway.
Everyone's staring at me,
everyone knows Mom OD'd.
Someone's baby is crying,
the police radio is blaring,
and people are talking about the nothing
they think they know.

But they're not dissing me, they're saying,
"Good game today, Ceti. We got you.
You'll pull through, honey. I'm sorry.
Hey, girl, it'll be all right.
Hey, baby, let me know what you need.
We're here for you. We got you—"

"Thank you," I say,
surprised they're not hating,
and I go down
to the seventh.

No sister, no mother.

But I know there's another
end—just don't know
how to get there.
I wish I did,

Nia is here.
"Do you want me to put a flower in your hair?"

> "Okay," I whisper. I wish
> I could stay here with her
> fingers kneading my hair.

Mom and I used to look for the dandelions
you could blow in the wind
and make a wish.

I can hear her now.
I did my best, Ceti.
What else can I do?
I laugh a little
cuz her best
blew away in the wind
a long time ago.

Dancing in the Light

Will's Mom tells me to sleep in Nia's room,
to call her Angie, and to make myself at home
because there's always room for one more.
She's frying spicy beef with onion and pepper,
and me, Ruby, and Will are sitting on Nia's bed.
But Mom's still taking all the space in my head.

I can see her in the fluorescent lights
of the hospital, writhing and kicking
like she's dancing in the spotlight.
Still getting all the attention,
while my whole world is crashing,
          down
                    again.

I want her out of my head.
Want her to go away like the photo
of us at the way bottom of my bag.

Will takes my hand.
"Hey, it's gonna be all right.
Even if it doesn't feel like it
                    right now."

If You Really Want to Be My Friend

Ruby says, "You have to talk to me, Ceti.
I mean, if you're really my friend."
"Us," Will says.
"Yeah, us," Ruby says.
"Me, too," Nia says from the doorway.
Will sighs. "Nia, can you get us something
to drink, like one of those fancy things
you make with the straws and flowers and stuff?"
"Okay!" she says,
and we laugh as Nia runs away.

It's a relief not to be hiding Mom anymore.
I thought they wouldn't want to hang out with me anymore.
I try to explain.
"My mom said if I said anything
to anyone they'd take her away.
I'd lose her, you know, forever."

"Right, I get it." Ruby nods. "It was so hard
when my mom was in rehab. But we're your friends.
We want to make things *better*."
Ruby leans closer.
"You won't lose us,
but you have to talk to us."
"Yeah, Ceti," Will adds. "We're here for you.
We got your back."

"Yeah." *Just have to figure out how to talk.*

They wait like they got all day.

“Okay, it’s just, um, not that easy.”

“Uh-huh.”
They nod.

“Everyone else seems so—normal. What could I say—
my mom almost burned the house down yesterday.
Or her arm was bleeding so bad
I thought I’d have to call 911 before Math.
Or I’m starving cuz there’s no food at my house,
only junkies—”

“Yeah, you *can* say that,” Ruby says.
‘Girl, *you* decide what to do.”

“It’s just that I keep thinking
it’s my fault—”

“You had to go to the game today,”
Will says. “Are you insane?
We woulda lost. And just saying,
but I really don’t think you could have stopped—”
“No way, Ceti.” Ruby stomps by me.
“Don’t even go there—that was all about her.
Like with my mom and her drinking,
it took me forever to realize it wasn’t my fault.”

“I just thought if she got clean
things could be like they used to be.”
I rub the inside of my palm.

“Yeah, I thought I could fix it, too.
By the way, you can stay with me too.”

Her house is too big, too rich.
I feel good here. Feel right.
Plus, I don't want her mom
to look at me like she looked at my mom.
"Thanks," I say. "I'll stay here tonight.
Can't really think past that."

"You have to play soccer,"
Will says. "Seriously,
soccer is freedom."

Soccer
is
freedom.
"Yeah, it is," I say.

"Yeah, it is."

Angie pokes her head in.
"Your mother is doing fine.
We can probably visit her tomorrow,
okay?"

I nod. "Thank you."

"Almost supper-time," she says.

Haven't heard that one for a while.
Smells so good, sweet and spicy.

"I better go," Ruby says.
"Hey, tomorrow's your birthday."

"Right. I forgot."

"What'd you want anyway?"
Will asks.

I look up at his posters.
"You can keep LeBron,
but Ronaldo's got to go."

He cracks up.
"Rematch tomorrow?"

"As long as you don't pretend to lose
because it's my birthday."

He straight up tackles me.
I hold in a scream,
the good kind.

"Now it's really time for me to go."
Ruby pushes her hair back.
"Talk tomorrow?"

"Okay."

"I mean it."

"I know."
Before she leaves, I tell her,
"You know what I really want?"

"What?"

"To have my friends
close by."

Stray Cat Blues

Nia is petting my hair
like I'm a cat—
a stray cat
in a new lair—
curled in a ball, warm and fed,
but scratching and clawing.
"Ceti," Angie says
from the kitchen.
"They're trying to locate
any of your relatives.
You have a grandfather,
right?"

"Yes."
Hope flutters up
to my throat,
and before I can stop it,
takes off flying.
"He used to live in Roosevelt Tower
in New York. But I haven't seen him
for a long time."
I breathe.
"I really want to."
Gramps.

"Okay," Angie says,
holding her phone.
"We'll see what we can do."

Sweet Black Angel

Nia leaves her light on at night.
I watch her sleeping on her side,
her mouth open a little,
braids out, her hair fluffy and kinked.
Her eyelashes, long and dark, flutter
and her skin smells like cocoa butter.
I touch her small, perfect chin
with my finger and she takes my hand
and tucks it under her cheek.
When my hand falls asleep,
I slip it out of hers.
            The white scars
on my palm shine translucent and deep.
Close my eyes, then my hand
over hers
again.

Lies

Wish those stupid white lines
would disappear right now.
Don't know what was truth—
and what was lies.

In Another Land

In my dream
of New Hampshire
the sky is blue
and clear like glass,
and we're running
through a field
of grass.
And I am holding
her hand.

How Can I Stop

Nia's gone,
but the warm print of her
is still there,
reminding me
of all that's missing.
I'm fifteen today,
and suddenly
a birthday memory
comes flooding back—of me
playing soccer behind La Viva.
Mom brought me leftover quesadilla,
chips and salsa.
One of the last days
she waitressed was the day
I turned double digits.
When we got back home,
she whipped eggs and butter,
and flour and sugar by hand
till she was sweating.
But she couldn't get
the lumps out
and it was way too sweet.
And we forgot to buy vanilla,
baking soda, and birthday candles.
She threw the bowl
and the batter splattered.

"It's okay, Mom," I told her.
"I like the frosting the best."
We ate her buttercream frosting

from the bowl.
"This is the best cake ever,"
I said, and she started to cry
and couldn't stop.
"Someday, Mom, we can make
a Disney castle cake, okay?"
She nodded. *Someday*
was going to be
the busiest day
ever.

Feels like a bullet's
lodged inside
my heart
right now.

Angie knocks on the door.
"Come in," I tell her.
Is she going to tell me Mom is dead?

A blue scarf on her head,
she says, "Good morning, Ceti.
And happy birthday!"

I love her face.

"Your mom had a hard night, honey.
So tomorrow's better to see her, okay?"

"Okay."

"Pancakes when you're ready."

"Angie, do you think I can stay
here one more day?"

"Longer than that!" Nia says
and jumps on the bed.
"Happy birthday, Ceti!"
Her fingers are sticky,
and she smells like maple syrup.
"Can you play soccer with me today?"

Wanna Hold You

Blueberry pancakes are fluffy
and soaked in syrup.
I'm on number three
when Will's dad comes in
and waves his hand at me.
"So you are the famous fútbol player
I heard about."

Will sighs. "Soccer, Dad.
It's soccer here."

My face goes hot. "I'm not famous."
Turns even redder realizing he was joking.
"I mean, not exactly Messi."

His dad has Will's wide smile.
Skin's darker and he's bald,
making his ears stick out a mile,
like Obama's.

"Thank you for letting me stay," I say.

When his soft brown eyes look at me,
I look down.
"Ceti, you are welcome here."

An ache presses through my chest.
It hurts so much—
I put my fork down and close my eyes.
Tears pour down my face.

"What's the matter, Ceti?"
Will's there, and Nia too.
No one knows what to do,
till Angie smooths out my hair.
She whispers, "It's okay now."
Nia looks confused. "Ceti,
did someone hurt your feelings?"

> "I'm sorry."
> I don't understand
> why he's so nice to me.
> He doesn't even know me.
> "It's cuz I do—feel—welcome,"
> I say between gulps of air.
> "And, um, the pancakes are really good."

They laugh.
Angie turns to the window to wipe her eyes.
"Let's play some soccer, okay?" Will says.
"We'll take on my dad. Right, Dad?"

"That sounds like a challenge,"
he says, patting his stomach.

Nia, Will, and I take my ball
to the field.

> "Okay," I tell Nia, "lock your ankle, then kick
> with your shoelaces or the inside of your foot."
> I tap my foot. "Do you know who Messi is?"

"I know who Ronaldo is."

> I roll my eyes.
> "Okay, we need to start from the beginning.
> Messi is the greatest soccer player in the world—"

Will grabs me around the shoulders.
"Take it back! Tell her who the best soccer player
in the world really is!"

"I did—Messi!"

He picks me off the ground.
"What'd you say?"

The sun warms my face
as I catch his eyes
and I know he's for real.
I mean, he likes me
the way I like him.
I know because I feel it
way deep inside.
It hurts in a good way
like it did at breakfast.
"Don't let go yet, okay?"

"I'm gonna hold you like this
till you admit Ronaldo's the best—"

"Or till your dad gets here—"

He groans and lets go in about a half a second,
smiling. "I'll get you later."

Nia runs to meet their dad.
"You're already huffing and puffing!
You're on Will's team—
girls against boys! Come on, Ceti,
you're on my team."

I have a team.

Going Home

Thing is, in soccer
it doesn't matter
who your mom or dad is,
but how you play the game.
And there is nothing
like the feeling of scoring
a goal.

After we play,
Will's dad lies
on the grass,
and can't get up.
"How did you do that?"
he asks me.
We all laugh.
He's a security guard.
Maybe that's why I feel
so safe.

Will says, "Come on,
let's go home."

He's talking to me.

Home.
Home.
Home.

I Am Waiting

Angie makes spaghetti and meatballs for supper.
Then we have chocolate cake with chocolate frosting.
They sing "Happy Birthday" to me.
"What're you gonna wish for, Ceti?"
"Yeah, make a wish, Ceti."

Truth is, I'm tired of waiting
for wishes to come true.
"I already got my wish today—
when the girls crushed the boys, 5 to 2."

"Oh yeah!" Nia calls.

"No fair," Will goes,
"I had a handicap!"

"Hey, I heard that,"
his dad says.

Angie brings out presents wrapped in tissue.
Two pairs of jeans, two T-shirts, both blue,
and a 100 percent cashmere hoodie, soft and pinkish gray.
I look up, like someone must have made a mistake—
I've never had anything this nice before—
and slip it on fast just in case.

"Some of the neighbors chipped in," Angie tells me.
"You look so pretty, Ceti."

I can hardly say thank you,

thinking this could all

disappear
in one, two, three—
goodbye—
like a joke, a trap,

like Will says, "Oh, snap!"

Out of Tears

Monday morning when I'm getting ready for school,
Angie tells me, "There're some complications
with your mom. Do you want to see her now?"

Stop.
"Can we go after school?"

"They think you should go now."
Angie's hair hangs over her shoulders,
dark and wavy on her blue scrubs.
She tilts her face, smooth and brown,
and says, "She's your mom."

"Does it mean I have to live
with her again?"

"It means you see her for twenty minutes,
that's all."

"Can you take me?"

"I'll be right outside the room the whole time,"
Angie says.

The whole way there in the car,
I think I'm going to be sick.
Hospital smell makes me sicker.
Angie puts her hand on my back
and tells me, "You're really brave, Ceti."

“I’m not,” I say.
“I’m not anything.”

“No,” she says fiercely,
holding me by the shoulders.
“You’re *everything*.
Do you hear me?”

I nod. Breathe
and walk into Mom’s room.

I swear that’s never gonna be me
lying in a bed with tubes and wires feeding me—
that’s not life.
That’s waiting to die.

Mom lays her skinny eyes on me.
“Get me outta here, Ceti,
please.”

I whisper, “I can’t do that, Mom.
You know that.”

“You got to help me.
It hurts so bad.”

“That’s why you’re here.
They’ll make you better.”

“I—need—to—get—out—”

I know that I-need-some voice.

She whimpers.
“Makes everything stop hurting.”

"'Cept me, Mom," I say.

"You're fine, I'm not."
She closes her eyes
and mumbles something like,
"I hate it in here.
Everyone looking at me
like I'm a junkie.
I'm freakin' fine,
I just need to get out.
Just need—"
She punches the bed.
"What am I supposed to do
with no money?
Do you have five dollars, Ceti?
Cheaper than a freakin'
six-pack for crissake."
Then she starts her kicking fit
all over again, crying.
"I'm your mother, Ceti.
You need to stay with me.
I can't lose you."

"I thought we were going to New Hampshire,
Mom. What happened to starting over
again? And, and—*Luna*?" I whisper.

"You think I don't have dreams, Ceti?
My mother put me on meds when I was eight.
She messed me up!"

I've heard it all before.
It's always about her.

She keeps blubbering
about how she's gonna change,
start over, take care of me.
Her voice is all scratchy.
Tears run down her face.

Seen it all before.
It's always about her.

"I'm going to rehab.
I mean it, I'm gonna do it."

She's crying for both of us.
"I can't lose you, Ceti.
I'm better than this. I really am.
You are mine—
that old bastard better not come
around either."

"Gramps?"

"Yeah, Gramps.
He lost his chances about thirty freakin' years ago."
She wipes her face on the sheets, points at me.
"I'm gonna get clean. You have to believe me."

We *were*   happy—

once.
I know it deep
down.
"I hope you do."

But whatever happens,
my dreams are not gonna die

with hers.

Breathe in—
and out.

"You have to believe me,"
she says again, new tears falling.

Sometimes words don't make
any difference at all.
I'm done with talking and crying.

"Please, Ceti,
I'm dying—"

"*Someday,*" I say softly,
"when you can be my mom again,
and not someone else."

Mom starts itching the scabs on her arms
till her fingernails are red.
Eyes are wild red and mad.
She turns her face away from me.
Screaming, "I did everything for you
and this is how you repay me—
this is what I get!"

Nurse runs in with Angie.

"I didn't do anything." I shake my head,
backing toward the door. "I swear it."

"I know," the nurse says like she's been there before.
"Go ahead now."
Mom's body shakes

so crazy I think she's faking.
Then she's finally—quiet.

Nurse says, "Go to school now, like a good girl."
She adds so soft I barely hear,
"You got your whole life ahead of you."

Let Me Go

In geometry class, everyone's looking at me.
I can't think about equations.
What does *x* equal when there's no *y* or *z*?
I wish there was a formula for me.
I'm like the variable without a calculation.

At lunch Ruby asks again, "Do you want to live
with us for a while—"

"Thanks," I say.
"You sure your mom's good with that?"

"Of course, Ceti."

But I feel her mother looking down on me.
Still, I might not have a choice—
cuz what about next week and the week after that?
What does *x* equal when it's the unknown
without a home?

Nurse Emi and a couple teachers stop by
to congratulate me on the finals.
Seems like about a hundred years ago.

Nurse Emi smiles.
"Do you need more vitamins to go?"

"Not anymore," I say. "I'm good."
But I'm not.

"Stop by whenever you want."

"Thank you."

Ruby isn't patient. She stares at me.
"Ceti, you better talk to me—
now."

I do. I tell her about Luna,
about how much I wanted
a sister.

Bell rings and she pushes her lunch away.
"Okay, come on, we're going outside
to do this right."

She pulls me out the side door into the November wind,
across the football and soccer fields.
"Here."
Ruby kneels on the leaves
by the edge of the trees,
her hair blowing all around.
She digs into the ground,
making a shallow hole.
Unclasps a silver cross
hanging on her necklace.
"This is for Luna."
Then she wraps the cross
inside a red and yellow leaf.
"Drugs mess you up so bad—
it's not fair. She didn't do anything!"
Ruby hands me the folded leaf.
"Do you want to say something?"

I shake my head.

All my words are swirling
away in the wind.

"You'd be the best sister in the world,
Ceti. Okay? Do you get that?"

I place the leaf in the ground.

"She'll be right here while you're playing,"
Ruby says. "Goodbye, Luna."
We fill the hole together.

"I wanted to be your sister," I whisper.
"Sorry you had to leave—
I mean, I know it wasn't your fault,
dying—
so I guess I'm saying goodbye
for now, okay, Luna?"
I hope I see you some time
somewhere, like in my dream

someday.

Shake Your Hips

We start back through the cold gray,
both of us quiet, shivering—

Ruby says, "Sometimes when I run out of words—"

"*You* run out of words?" I interrupt.

She punches me in the arm.
"As I was saying, when I run out of words,
I dance, cuz it always makes me feel better.
I remember your mom dancing. She was good."

"It's weird," I say. "I know that Luna died,
and Foxface, but it feels like my mom did too.
Like she's dead."

"Yeah. Yeah, I get that,"
Ruby says carefully.
"So, when I'm scared
and don't wanna be,
I sometimes do this."
Ruby shakes her hips.
"You know, like this.
Makes me feel better,
shakes all the bad stuff away."
She swivels her hips,
shakes her arms,
thrusts and turns,
tosses her hair.
Waits for me to join.

"I know you got it in you, girl.
Come on, shake those tears away.
No one's gonna see you out here!"
She takes my hands
and twirls me around,
grinds up next to me,
shaking her hips even harder.
I laugh a little,
sway my body just a little,
listen for her beat,
then hop and skip,
feeling like, next to her,
I can do anything.

"Yeah, like that," Ruby says.
"Gotta feel it. Nothing to be afraid of,
just move. Yeah, and say it.
Say you can do anything.
You *are* anything you wanna be,
Ceti.
I'm not leaving till you say it."

I remember what Angie said.
You're everything. Do you hear me?

Not nothing.

Not nothing.

Not nothing.

Feel Ruby's hand warm in mine.
Kinda like my dream
of me and Mom running
in the field—
except this is for real.
"You got this," Ruby says.
"Now tell me

you're someone."

"I'm someone."

"Louder!"

"I'm someone!"

"One more time."

"I'm someone!

Okay?"

"Okay."

Like a Rolling Stone

Back in school,
I'm a *Walking Dead* zombie
for the rest of the day.
Everything is temporary.
Not sure where I'll go next.
Seems like everyone else has a home.
Feels like no one really knows
what it's like to be this alone.
Mom used to say she was like a rolling stone
cuz she was on her own.
Maybe it started thirty years ago
when Gramps left, or Gran put her on pills.
Maybe that's my fate too,
but I don't want to be on my own.
I need a home.

It's Not Easy

Right before last period,
Will pulls me into the auditorium.
It's dark and empty in the last row.
He says, "You know it's been torture
having you staying with us."

"What's that supposed to mean
exactly?"

He leans closer,
lifts my chin.
"Means I like you,
exactly."

"Okay."

He takes my hand,
turns it over, and runs his finger
along the lines of my palm.
"I know it's been hard."

"Yeah."

A tear escapes my eye,
starts to slide down my cheek.
He catches it with his lips,
then his mouth finds mine,
salty and sweet.

Cool, Calm & Collected

Later that afternoon, Angie sits me down.
"Your coach called. She has an extra room—
she wants you to stay."

"Like, I'd *live* with *Coach*?"

"Everything else would stay the same—
school, soccer, and such."

"But—*Coach*?"

"Yes." Wisps of dark hair peek through
the blue flowered scarf on Angie's head.

My head
spins.
I know I need to go
somewhere.

"You better come back every Sunday,
because we have to get their dad back in shape
somehow."

"Would it be just for now?"

"For now, and later if you want.
She said you could visit.
Will and Nia can come too."

"Okay, I'll visit."

I don't know why I never imagined
Coach having a life off the field.
Her house is yellow with a fenced-in yard.
A big scruffy dog named Lincoln,
gray, black, and brown,
pounces and licks our faces and hands.
Nia screams and runs, and Will falls back a step,
but I hold on to that fur ball
cuz he's warm and sloppy wet.
"He likes you," Coach says.

Must be my lucky day—
that's two times today.

Then Coach opens her front door,
shows me the room on the second floor
with glow-in-the dark stars covering the ceiling and walls.
Through the window are trees, a soccer net, and balls.

"Oh man, you're so lucky," Will says.

"Is this really yours?" Nia asks.

"If Ceti wants, she can stay here,
and you can visit her any time."

"What about me?" Will asks.

"You can, too." Coach laughs.
"But downstairs."

Angie calls, "Thank you."

> (*Can't be true, can't be true, can't be true.*
> *It's all too good to be true. But it is.*)

"Um, should I still call you Coach?"

"How about Kate?" she says.

"Okay. And could Lincoln sleep in here—with me?"

"I think he'd like that. He's bored of me."

In the living room, there are pictures of a girl
not much older than me, holding a soccer ball.

"Who's this?" Nia asks.

"It was my daughter." Kate smiles a little
but doesn't explain.
"What do you think, Ceti?"

"Good."

"How about staying tomorrow?"

"Okay."

All of a sudden, I have somewhere to go—
a dog, a room, a home.
Still can't understand why they're all being so nice.
But what I'm thinking is:
Only one more night at Angie's.

Free

Angie's been on the phone since we got back.
When she finally sets it down,
I ask her if there's anything I can help with.
"Seriously?" Will moans. "What're you doing?
"You're messing with the standards around here."

Angie smiles.
"You could introduce Will to the washer and dryer."

He punches my arm. "Nice one, Ceti."

I shrug and we each take a side of the laundry basket
and walk it down the hallway to the elevator.

Soon as the door opens, I smell him—
the fresh tar, smoke, and filth—
nothing sweet about this smell
he left behind each time.
Sugarman stares hard at me.
My insides go cold, remembering
Mom crazed and crying, begging
for his powder, his smack.
He flips his thin greasy hair back.
Jean jacket, black-stained workboots,
thin lips, long nose—I catch him glancing
at the number 7 button before we head down.

"What the hell happened up there?"
he says.

I make myself look into his red eyes.
"What'd you want?" I say.

"Nuthin'. You never saw me."
The elevator *dings* and he knocks past me
into the black night.

"I *wish* I never saw you," I say.

"He makes the other guy look nice."
Will holds my hand.
"Free at last?"

"Yeah, later, Sugarman."
Open my eyes to the bright lights and smile.
"Free except from the laundry."

Till the Next Goodbye

After Nia goes to sleep,
I take the photo of Mom and me
out of the bottom of my bag.
Glass is broken, but the picture is there.
It's real—me and her.
It was supposed to be like that again—
with fields of grass, a horse to ride,
and enough stars to fill the whole sky.
Except that it wasn't.
That's the truth
I have to remember.
Maybe another day,
another life.

Stop Breaking Down

The next week after school,
some kids are pointing at the street corner
where Mom is freaking out like a fool.
They laugh and whistle as she dances a little.
"Hey, come on over here and get some," she sings.
"I got some sugar for all you sweet things."
She laughs when they laugh
like they're laughing together.

Want to say, *Please, Mom, not here.*
I think I'm going to be sick.
For the last few years,
my heart has been breaking
slllooooowwwwwlllly—
now it suddenly snaps in two.
I break it this time between

Mom	and me.
Sorry, Mom,	I have to.
Like she's seeing inside	me, even though I'm hiding,
she yells, "I'm going to wait	for you, Ceti
I'll be here *forev*—"	I don't stay—I take off
	running
	in the other direction
	where
	Life
	Life
	Life

Life
Life
Life
Life
Life
Life
Life
Life
Life
Life
Life
is.

Respectable

It's so quiet at Kate's yellow house,
at night Lincoln's the only one who makes noise.
Sometimes he whimpers and cries in his sleep.
I think it's because I've been telling him my story,
the one about me.
          I'm getting better at talking,
          even if he's the only one who knows everything.

It's so quiet at Kate's yellow house,
except when the wind blows against my windows,
and the branches scrape and knock,
and I think Mom and Sugarman have found me.
They call my name into the night, *Ceti, Ceti—*
Mom's face is so sad, I can't bear to look at her,
but if I go closer, she laughs and scratches
the glass. Then I hide in Lincoln's patches
of brown scruff and wait for the light to come.

It's so quiet at Kate's yellow house,
and it smells like melted butter and sugar—
it's hard to believe this is normal.
In the kitchen, Kate goes barefoot
and wears her long hair down,
makes chocolate chip cookies,
and lets me eat the batter.
She says she'll take me to see Mom
when I'm ready—
I don't know if I'll ever be *ready.*
She tells me the scout wants to see me play
again, and I'm sure she's kidding

cuz so many good things just don't happen
to me.

It's so quiet at Kate's yellow house,
I can hear Lincoln shaking his head when Kate asks him,
"Would I ever joke about something like that?"
I swear he flops his shaggy face side to side.
Kate says, "See?"

It's so quiet at Kate's yellow house,
I have to keep telling myself *it's real*—
Mom used to say,
"One day I'll be respectable.
Just you wait and see."
One day, I hope that will be you,
Mom, and I can see you
again.
In the meantime,
I think I found *someday*—
            even if it is only temporary—
Mom, it's so quiet in Kate's yellow house.

Can You Hear the Music

Almost two weeks after
Foxface and Mom OD'd,
there's a pick-up game
at the old school field,
so that's where we're heading—
Ruby, Will, Nia, and me.
The wind is November cold,
almost Thanksgiving.
Last year Mom was so high
she forgot what day it was.
Even though everything's changed,
still seems like something's
missing,
a hole
where there should be
something that's my own.
It's like I'm swirling
in some current way out of my control,
trying to understand how I got here
how the pieces fit together
to make me
Ceti.

I hear them before I see them playing
and run ahead, feeling that pull—
can't stop myself, no way.
Yank my hair into a ponytail,
then I'm flying down the wing—
roll it back, give and go, dribble in,
dribble out, *score*!

This is freedom.

I don't even see Kate watching
with Angie, who's standing
in her scrubs behind
a wheelchair with an old man
till goal number three.
He's waving his hands wildly,
          looking at me.
Wipes his face with his sleeve—
maybe it's the wind making him cry.
"Ceti girl!" he calls.

Stop.

Only one person ever called me that.
Someone turns up the music on the speaker.
Maybe I didn't hear it right.
"Ceti girl, say hi to your old Gramps."

          Gramps.
          It's really him.

He's why I'm playing soccer right now.
I know cuz I feel it—
the magic—ringing in my ears—
like music.
He loves me more than anything.

Angie is smiling,
and Will is telling me,
"Go, I got you—"
and I know that magic is mine
cuz I'm running

high.

ACKNOWLEDGEMENTS

A million thanks to my brilliant agent, Sally Wofford-Girand. And my shooting star of an editor, Jaynie Royal, Pam Van Dyk, and everyone at Regal House Publishing, the best home a girl could ask for.

I am indebted to my treasured readers: Vanessa Diffenbaugh, Leah DeForest, Talaya Delaney, Maria Kiely, and my beloveds, Tess, Cece, and Chris Walsh.

And thank you to my best homebases-away-from-home: Kate Canfield, Nora Love, Sue Miller, Kyra and Coco Montagu, and Sef and Maren Stever-Kloninger.

For all those who have supported me along the way with their love and generosity, thank you: My family, especially Mary Sullivan, Liz Hurley, Ann McCarthy, Marcia Garvey, Chuck Sullivan, Katy Morgan, and Kay Walsh. Social media consultant extraordinaire, Calla Walsh. And Malcolm Walsh, who makes me happy every day.

A special thanks to Cambridge Youth Soccer for all they do to get kids on the field every season.

And in memory of Jim Zinn for showing us how to live our dreams—and to Frankie Thompson and Sophia Zinn with love.

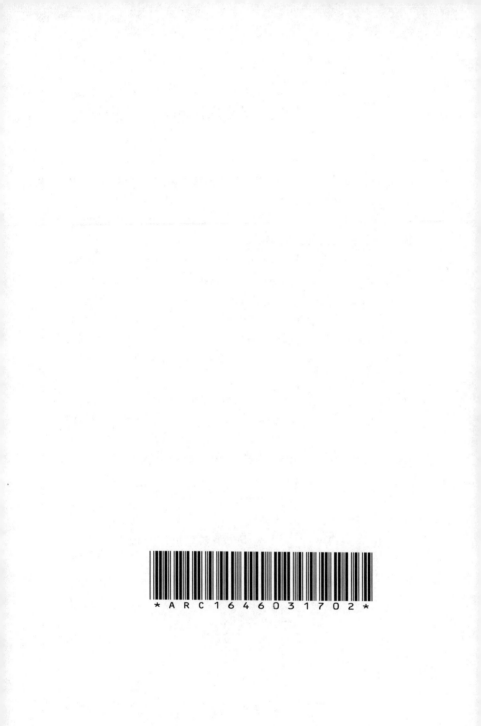